MIND*STORMS*

STORIES TO BLOW YOUR MIND

Neal Shusterman

TOR ®

A TOM DOHERTY ASSOCIATES BOOK
NEW YORK

This is a work of fiction. All the characters and events portrayed in this book are either products of the author's imagination or are used fictitiously.

MINDSTORMS: STORIES TO BLOW YOUR MIND

Cover art by Robert Papp

A Tor Book
Published by Tom Doherty Associates, Inc.
175 Fifth Avenue
New York, NY 10010

Tor® is a registered trademark of Tom Doherty Associates, Inc.

ISBN: 0-812-55198-2

First edition: November 1996

Printed in the United States of America

0 9 8 7 6 5 4 3 2 1

To the Fictionaires,
who are *so* talented it's scary . . .

Acknowledgments

I'd like to thank everyone whose efforts have brought this particular storm to shore.

Many thanks to Terry Black for his invaluable contribution to Midnight Michelangelo; to Veronica Castro, for her tireless hours of work; to Elaine, Brendan, and Jarrod for a universe of inspiration; and to Jonathan Schmidt, Kathleen Doherty, and everyone at Tor books, who are the wings above my wind.

CONTENTS

● ●

PACIFIC
RIM

● ●

YOUR ESCAPE BEGINS HERE.

The sign on the door of the travel agency screams out the words in bold purple letters. I want to believe it, because escape is something I desperately need. So does Mom. Ever since Dad left, Mom's been going on and on about taking a real vacation. Europe maybe, or an African safari.

"I want to do something on the edge," Mom keeps saying, "something special."

I'm all for it. After all, I've lived my whole life in Phoenix, and the farthest away I've ever been was a vacation in Disneyland, which wasn't too adventurous, if you know what I mean. So anything that involves passports and places where they don't speak English would be the best thing as far as I'm concerned.

So Mom and I walk into the travel agency, all wide-eyed

and gawking, ready to see the world. The place makes me feel like we're already on vacation. Colorful balloons are suspended everywhere, and loud Caribbean music fills the air with such a contagious beat that I feel like doing the limbo. The staff are all wearing bright Hawaiian shirts, and the walls are plastered with exotic destinations so beautiful that I want to visit every single one of them.

A woman with perfect hair, perfect teeth, and earrings much too big steps up to greet us. "Welcome to Lifetime Travel," she purrs. "How can I help you?"

"We want a vacation," my mom says. "Something *different*."

The travel agent snaps open a drawer and pulls out one brochure after another. "How many will be traveling?"

My mom tries to hide the pain the question brings, but her pursed lips and sorrowful eyes tell all. "Just me and my son, right, Alex?"

I force a weak smile, and the woman looks away. She can't know all the things that happened between Mom and Dad before he left, but she knows enough not to ask any more questions. I suppose she dealt with shattered families like ours before, trying to find a vacation that will somehow, magically, fix everything.

The travel agent fans out the brochures like they're an oversized deck of cards, babbling on about prices and meal plans—but I can tell Mom's not listening. Something's caught her eye. There on the corner of the desk, a brochure sticks out—something the woman didn't seem anxious to show us. There's enough of it visible to show the bow of a boat. Mom pulls it out from beneath the pile. On the cover is a cruise ship, tall and wide, with a least a dozen decks. It's a magnificent thing, with a shiny white hull and ocean-green portholes.

Bright letters across the top of the brochure read PACIFIC RIM CRUISES. The name of the ship is the *Heavenward*. The pages of the brochure are filled with happy people swimming and dancing and eating, in a kind of splendor I can barely even imagine.

The travel agent eyes us warily. "Oh, you don't want that," she says, waving it off. "It's . . . uh . . . out of your price range."

My mother snaps her eyes up. "How would *you* know what our price range is?"

"Well . . . uh . . . I mean, I just don't *recommend* it." She quickly digs into another drawer. "If it's cruises you want, I can book you on dozens of others."

But Mom holds her ground. "Tell us about this one."

The woman looks to Mom, then to me, then reluctantly begins to speak as Mom and I leaf through the brochure.

"The *Heavenward* is a new ship," says the woman, "from a new and inexperienced cruise line. . . ."

I raise my eyebrows. "Says here it's the largest cruise ship ever built."

"A hundred and twenty tons," says the woman. "But—"

"And where does it cruise to?" asks Mom, cutting her off.

"Nowhere yet. Its maiden voyage isn't until next month."

I can tell that Mom's frustrated by the way this woman doesn't quite answer her question, so we find the answer in the brochure ourselves. Mom's eyes widen happily.

"A cruise to the Orient!" Mom says.

"Yes—to the Far East," says the travel agent, as if there's a difference.

According to the brochure, the *Heavenward* will depart from Honolulu and sail west across the Pacific, bound for Japan, China, and Thailand. A three-week cruise with ten ports of call!

I look up from the brochure and catch Mom's eyes. They are tne same eyes she had when she saw that painting in the art gallery. The one that cost way too much . . . and then two days later ended up in our living room.

The travel agent must see that look in my mom's eyes, too.

"I should explain something about Pacific Rim Cruises," says the travel agent in a calm, calculated voice, as if she's trying to talk someone in from the edge of a building. "They've built a magnificent ship . . . but they *don't know much about world travel.* This cruise that they're doing . . . it's going a little *too* far . . ."

"Nothing's too far for me," says Mom. "The farther the better."

The woman pales a bit, and I realize that she isn't trying to be rude. She's trying to warn us of something . . . something she wouldn't dare speak aloud . . .

But Mom doesn't care much for warnings. So she pulls out a wad of credit cards the size of a bar of soap. "We're taking that maiden voyage," Mom says. "Best room available. Money is no object."

And so the travel agent has no choice but to give us what we want.

It begins on July fourth. A flight to Honolulu, a taxi ride to the port, and there we are—staring at the *Heavenward*—a majestic white giant, impossibly huge. The ship fills up my whole mind when I look at it, leaving no room for other thoughts.

Everything on board is perfect, from our stateroom filled with luxurious wood and polished brass, to the nine-story atrium in the middle of the ship, where four glass elevators ride up and down. It's hard to believe this is all on a ship! There's even an entire kid deck filled with video games, pizza places, and just about anything else a kid could dream of. I now know why they named the ship the *Heavenward*, because as far as I'm concerned, it's like I've died and gone to heaven.

It's during that first evening at the midnight buffet that I see the strange old man.

He's in the kitchen—I catch glimpses of him every few moments through the swinging kitchen door. He's not a passenger, but a member of the crew. I don't think he's a cook, because he's not dressed like the rest of the kitchen workers. He wears a rumpled Hawaiian shirt that has seen better days, and his face is covered with beard stubble so dense that even the sharpest of razors would shy away from it. He seems out of place here, with a way about him too dark and brooding for a fun-filled cruise like this.

I can't get his face out of my mind, and even though I pile my plate high with food, I begin to lose my appetite. The old man's eyes seem worn and worried, and for some strange reason, I get the very clear sense that I should be worried, too.

Two days out of Hawaii, with wild parties raging on every deck, I get tired of the all-you-can-eat ice cream parlor, the free video games, and the dance-till-you-drop teen club. There's only so much pleasure a person can stand. So after dinner, I decide to explore.

Ships are great for secret exploration. They're like mazes filled with hallways and dim corners, and everywhere on the great ship you can hear the eerie rumble of the huge engine somewhere down below.

Finding the engine room is my goal. Sure, I could take the engine room tour, but it's much more fun to find it myself and be there when I'm not allowed.

On the lowest passenger deck I come to a door with a sign that reads NO ADMITTANCE, and I admit myself. Suddenly the luxurious beauty of the ship gives way to a dull beige corridor lined with the crew's quarters. I push farther and find a set of stairs leading down. I take it deck after deck after deck, deep into the bowels of the ship, wandering aimlessly through narrow access-ways until I finally stumble upon the engine room.

You'd think the engine room of a great ship like the *Heavenward* would have a huge crew of engineers—but a ship as sophisticated as this must practically run itself. There's only one man on shift. A man I recognize.

It's the old man from the kitchen the night before.

He turns his weary eyes to me. He has an intense gaze, and now that I get a better look at him, I can tell that he's an educated man by he way he carries himself—as if the crushing weight of some secret knowledge hunches his shoulders, like Atlas holding up the world. The shadows are deep here, and in those shadows his face seems cragged and cracked, like the Grand Canyon seen from an airplane. I can see that he's not so much old as he is worn. Worn and tired.

"You don't belong here, boy," he says. "Go back up. Party while you can." His words give me a shiver that rises up my spine, but I force it back down.

Around us the engine roars, and through an iron catwalk I can see the silver cylinder of a propeller shaft leading to the stern. Beneath that, the two sides of the hull come together, like an attic turned upside down. It reminds me that no matter how huge this thing is, it's just a boat, with miles of ocean beneath it. The thought unsettles me, and suddenly I want to be anywhere but the engine room.

"Uh . . . sorry," I say, "I took a wrong turn." I spin and hurry off, fully prepared to spend the rest of my cruise playing free video games, swimming, and eating myself into blimpdom.

But the old engineer calls out to me.

"Hold on there, Alex!" he says.

The ship lurches beneath me, making my stomach feel

queasy. Or maybe it's just the fact that the old man knows my name. I can't figure how he'd know it.

I turn, and he grins mysteriously. "The name's Riley," he says. "Third engineer. C'mon, I'll take you back to the passenger decks."

Soon the roar of the engines is far away once again. We wind down the narrow corridors and up flights of stairs, until reaching a doorway. Beyond the door I can hear the sound of distant partying; thousands of people drinking in a lifetime's worth of good times. As if there's no tomorrow.

It's then that I realize that I'm wearing my Little League shirt, with my name plastered right across the back. *Idiot!* I think. That's how he knew my name. All at once, that sick feeling twisting through my gut goes away. I feel normal again, until Engineer Riley puts his hand on the doorknob and turns to me. "Is this your first cruise?" he asks.

"Yes . . ."

He shakes his head. "I'm so sorry for you." Then he swings the door wide into the bright lights of the Aloha Deck.

The next morning we're still at sea, somewhere between Hawaii and Japan . . . or so the map in our brochure says. The ocean stretches out around us, featureless and flat, and although there are a hundred things for me to do today, I can't get Riley's face out of my mind. I can't forget the sorrowful way he looked at me when he opened that door . . . and what he said.

It takes me half the morning searching the ship, but finally I find him. Once again, I'm in a place I'm not supposed to be: the crew's recreation deck. It's a large space at the back of the ship, with a ceiling so low it feels like I'm being crushed between two decks. The large U-shaped room has wide portholes open to the sea, beyond which the white trail of the ship's wake disappears toward the horizon.

Riley's sitting alone, drinking his coffee steaming black. He doesn't seem surprised to see me; he just nods a weary greeting.

"That was a lousy thing to say to me yesterday," I tell him.

He knows exactly what I'm talking about. "You think that now, but you won't tomorrow," he answers.

"What's that supposed to mean?"

He takes a long time to answer. "How much have you traveled?" he asks.

"A lot," I lie. "I've been all over the world."

"Ever known a pilot, or the captain of a ship, boy?"

I shake my head, and he leans in closer to me and whispers, *"There's things they know . . . that regular people aren't supposed to know."*

"Like what?" I dare to ask.

Instead of answering me, he stands up and goes to one of the huge portholes. I follow him.

"What do you see when you look out there?" he asks.

"Nothing. Just the horizon."

"And what does the horizon look like to you?"

I shrug. "A line," I tell him. "A straight line."

He nods. "That's exactly right—and why is that?"

I begin to get annoyed. It's as if he's giving me a test. As if he thinks I don't know the answer, which I do.

"The curvature of the Earth," I tell him. "The Earth slopes off, and you can't see past the horizon."

Then he looks at me with those yellow, weary eyes.

"That's what they want you to believe," he says.

His words strike me like a blast of radiation. I can tell I've been hit by something major . . . but I don't feel it just yet. But I know I will. Somehow I sense that his words have created some immense damage in me, that will soon get much, much worse.

"Soon everything you know," he explains, "everything you believe in will crumble away."

I feel panic looming inside me like a storm. What he is trying to tell me begins to dawn on me.

I suddenly think of a silly drawing I once saw in history class: the world was a flat disk on the back of a giant tortoise. It was an example of an ignorant belief of people a thousand years ago. People who didn't know any better.

"You're . . . you're joking, right?" I ask him.

Riley says nothing, and I begin to get mad. "I suppose now you're going to tell me that we're all on the back of a turtle, and every time the turtle moves there's an earthquake."

Riley ponders it. I can't believe it—he actually takes me seriously! "I don't know about a turtle," he says finally. "But anything's possible."

As I look out over the flat immensity of the ocean, I become furious—because no matter how impossible what he's saying sounds, there's a part of me that might actually believe him. Not the rational, sensible part of me, but the part that knows no logic. The same part that makes me check under my bed every night, even though I haven't believed in monsters since I was five. I fight to keep down the breakfast that still stuffs my stomach.

"But if the world's not round . . . then how do you get to Japan and the Far East?" I ask.

He looks out toward the straight line of the horizon, worry coming back to his face. "Not the way we're going," he answers.

He breaks his gaze away from the porthole, as if unable to look at the ocean anymore, and moves away. I have to admit I feel the same. In my mind, the horizon, as calm as it is, seems razor sharp, and filled with terrifying unknowns.

Riley takes a big gulp of his cooling coffee.

"Sailors are a secretive bunch," he says. "We keep the nature of the world to ourselves—and you'd be amazed how easy it is to keep a secret when most everyone in the world already believes it. . . ." Then he sighs. "But sometimes the secret is kept too well . . . and every once in a while the wrong people build ships . . . like the people who run Pacific Rim Cruises. This is their first ship . . . and they just don't know . . ."

And then he grabs me by the shoulder, forcing me to look into his eyes. Forcing me to listen.

"When the time comes," he says, *"go to the back of the ship, no matter what they tell you."*

He downs the rest of his coffee, then abruptly tells me I should leave—but before I leave I have to ask him something.

"Riley," I ask, "if we're not headed toward Japan, where *are* we headed?"

He looks down at his empty cup, refusing to look me in the eye. "You don't want to know."

For the rest of that day, I weave in and out of the happy crowds of vacationers, but can't feel like one of them. They are already ghosts.

As the sun begins to cast long shadows across the deck, I find my mother stretched out in a lounge chair, reeking of suntan lotion and sipping an exotic drink the color of antifreeze.

When she sees me, she smiles and says lazily, "Let's never go back. Let's just float out here forever."

Although I know she's kidding, her words bring my last meal swimming toward high tide.

"Mom," I tell her, "I don't think this trip was a good idea."

She looks at me as if I've doused her with ice water. "Aren't you having a good time, Alex? There's so much to do—so many kids your age!"

I look toward the pool to see dozens of kids laughing and swimming and flying down the winding slide. I wish I could join in the fun, but the old man's crazy words strangle all hopes of enjoying myself.

"Just wait until we get to Japan," Mom reassures me. "I promise you, this trip will be something to remember!"

It happens that night.

During dinner, the seas become rough—the ship rolling and pitching so violently that Mom's lobster flies right into her lap.

I figure we must be in a terrible storm, but when I look out the window at the twilight sky, there are no clouds. Still the waves crash angrily against the ship with all the furious power the ocean can muster.

It's as if something is trying to make us turn back, I think, but I swallow the thought with my dinner roll.

I go to my cabin early, trying to sleep off my worry, but it's no use. All I can think about is the old engineer.

What Riley had said is impossible. More than impossible, it's inconceivable—it would mean a conspiracy too immense to be imagined. All the pilots, all the astronomers, all the astronauts—anyone who ever had the chance to truly study the Earth would know. Why would all those people keep it from the rest of the world?

Yet even as I think about it, I know the answer.

Because everything would fall apart.

The whole world would become a bottomless pit of fear and confusion if we suddenly realized we knew *nothing* about the true nature of the universe. We would be lost and helpless if, after all we thought we knew . . . we suddenly discovered . . . that the Earth was flat.

BAM! CRRRUNCH!

I'm suddenly thrown out of bed by the ship's violent lurch. There's no mistaking the meaning of that tearing, metallic sound, and I can already see in my mind the huge gash torn in the side of the ship.

Torn by what? I think. *We're out in the middle of the ocean. It can't be an iceberg—we're too far south.*

The ship's alarms clang in my ears so violently that every thought is blasted from my mind. I can hear my mother screaming, tumbling out of her bunk and banging her shin against the dresser.

Then another jolt throws us to the floor as a second hole is ripped in the hull.

We burst out into a hallway already packed with terrified passengers, and I remember Riley's words.

Go to the back of the ship.

All around us, people push toward the front of the ship, toward their muster stations, because that's what they were told in the lifeboat drill when we first came on board. That's where the closest staircase is.

But I grab Mom's hand and pull her against the crowd, until we join the people heading toward the stairwell at the back of the great ship.

We stumble our way up three flights of stairs to the promenade deck, and only now, as we are pushed against the railing, do we see the nature of the ship's ruin.

The *Heavenward* is wedged between giant crags of rock, massive gray granite slabs that jut up around us on either side. I know that these rocks aren't supposed to be here. We're out in the middle of nowhere, a thousand miles from Japan! I'm pretty certain that there's no map in the world that shows this granite reef.

Caught between the rocks, the back half of the ship is rocked violently by powerful waves . . . but the front end of the ship has a very different problem.

I watch in helpless terror as passengers cram into a forward lifeboat. As the lifeboat is lowered into the water I hear them scream . . . *because there is no water at the front of the ship.* There is no ocean. The crowded lifeboat tumbles into an emptiness as deep as the sky is high.

We have reached the edge of the earth.

I instantly realize what's about to happen. I'd done enough exploring to know that two of the ship's three main stairwells are toward the bow—and only one toward the stern. That means that at least two-thirds of the passengers are flooding the front half of the ship!

It only takes a minute for the weight of the ship to shift forward, off its delicate balance. I feel the ship tilting over the edge, and I scream. Then a hand firmly pushes me from behind. The railing before me gives way and I fall, but instead of landing in the ocean . . . I land in the shell of a lifeboat. People pile on top of me. My mother, and dozens of others.

We are lowered to the water. When I look up, I don't see the side of the ship, but instead see a propeller four times my height, churning the air uselessly.

"Hold on!" a voice shouts. A familiar voice. I turn back to see the weathered face of the third engineer. Riley releases the lifeboat from the crane, and it drops five feet to the surface of the roiling ocean. We narrowly miss being shredded by another propeller coming up through the water as the ship continues to tilt forward.

"We're all going to drown!" shouts my mother, out of her

mind with panic—but even in the rough waters of the great Pacific Rim, the small lifeboat manages to stay afloat.

Riley starts the engine and maneuvers us toward the granite reef that holds the ocean back. A wave deposits us on the shore.

"We'll climb to that ledge." Riley says, pointing to a rock plateau about ten feet above us. "The sea will be calm by morning."

Soaked and terrified, we all climb to the plateau, but I don't stop. I keep climbing, even though Riley tries to call me back. I climb as high as I can, until I come to the top of the ridge and can see everything.

They say you're not supposed to look at awful sights—that you should turn your eyes from things that shouldn't be seen. But no one has ever accused me of doing the right thing. I have to watch it happen.

From where I am, the sight is more incredible than anything I've ever seen, or ever will see again. The great granite reef of the Pacific Rim stretches as far as the eye can see in every direction. For the most part it holds back the sea, but it's filled with many cracks, through which the ocean pours like massive waterfalls spilling off the world into infinity.

The *Heavenward* is wedged in the throat of one of those waterfalls.

I stare in numb silence as the largest cruise ship ever built teeters forward like a seesaw and finally flips off the edge of the earth.

I keep my eyes locked on the ship as it tumbles end over end, down into a darkness speckled with stars. Soon I have to squint to see it. It seems no larger than a toothpick spinning in the void. And then a tiny point of light getting harder and harder to see.

When I turn, I see Riley standing behind me, and I pound his chest with my fists, almost slipping off the edge and into oblivion. "Why?" I scream. "Why didn't you stop the ship? Why didn't you turn us back?"

Riley grabs my flailing hands and looks me in the eye. "Because I didn't know if I believed it myself . . . until I really saw it."

He turns and looks out over the edge, squinting his eyes into the dark sky below, but the *Heavenward* is gone, with no sign that it ever existed at all. "Maybe it *needs* to happen every now and again," says Riley. "Maybe it needs to happen so that we never completely forget. . . ."

Far to the east, the dim light of the coming dawn paints the horizon a rich shade of blue, as the handful of us wait to be rescued. Below us, our lifeboat has long since been smashed to driftwood, but Riley is certain we'll be rescued—and sure enough, as day arrives, I can see the specks of rescue ships in the distance.

Perhaps it's just shock, but as I huddle with my mom to keep warm, the terror of what I witnessed slowly begins to turn to amazement. I can't help but wonder what the people on board the *Heavenward* saw as they fell from the world . . . but I suppose some secrets will never be known.

I look at the survivors around me and realize that we have all become inheritors of the secret. I know none of these people will ever tell, just as surely as I know that I never will—for if we did, the world would see us locked up as lunatics rather than ever consider the possibility that what we say is true.

How long has this been going on? I wonder. How many generations, and how many shipwrecks ago? But I doubt even Riley knows those answers.

"Are there other things?" I ask Riley. "More mysteries that people don't know?"

He smiles broadly and says, "Have you ever been to Nepal?"

I smile back at him, realizing exactly what he means—because I know my geography.

As I wait for the rescue ships to arrive, I think about my next great excursion. Not a trip of escape, but one of exploration. It may not be next year, or the year after that, but I know that someday I'll travel to Nepal—the gateway to the Himalayas—and Mount Everest, the highest mountain in the world.

There are people who call that place "the Roof of the World."

We'll see about that. . . .

I OF THE
STORM

●●

A late afternoon wind ushered in the sudden downpour. I could see the courtyard of the museum beginning to flood, while up above, lightning volleyed angrily across the clouds.

"Rainy season," Mom said. "It rains for an hour or two most afternoons this time of year."

"It's a good thing," Dad added. "It cleans up some of the smog."

I watched through a fogging window as the dark cumulus clouds slid past one another—and it seemed to me that they were closer than the storm clouds back home in Florida. I asked my parents about it.

"Of course they're closer," Dad said in his best know-it-all voice. "Mexico City's a mile and a half above sea level—that much closer to the clouds."

A wind swooped down and rattled the plate-glass window. I backed away, and Dad chuckled. "Ashley, this museum's stood through countless earthquakes. You don't have to worry about a little wind."

He turned and glanced at the gallery behind us. Giant Olmec heads with no bodies sat on pedestals beside sandstone sun wheels and weathered Aztec statues. It must have been what all the ancient civilizations did: carve these statues—because the museum was filled with gallery after giant gallery of massive carved stones.

"Where's your brother?" Dad asked me. "Weren't you keeping an eye on him?"

I heard my brother Jackson's giggle and the pattering of feet somewhere deep in the gallery.

"Don't play games, you two," Mom said, as if I was an accomplice to Jackson's mischief. "We have to get through the whole museum before five." Dad took a last look over the room to see if there was anything he'd missed, then he and Mom went on to the next gallery. Our tour schedule only allowed us three hours at Mexico City's Museum of Anthropology. And my parents were slaves to schedules.

Unfortunately, my life had been ruled by a very different clock lately. One that measured time in tantrums. It was a sugar-powered clock named Jackson.

Three years old, and about as disagreeable as a human can be, my brother Jackson lived by no schedule but his own, and right now, following Mom and Dad was not part of his agenda. He was nowhere in sight.

"Jackson?"

I heard him giggle again—farther away this time.

"Jackson, c'mon. Mom and Dad already left."

"Come and get me!" His voice echoed around the stones, and I couldn't tell where it came from.

"Fine. I'm leaving," I threatened, and turned, pretending to head off toward the next gallery. But I couldn't really leave him because Mom and Dad would be furious with me—as if it was my job to take care of Jackson.

"Ashley, take Jackson to the park."

"Ashley, put Jackson to bed."

"Ashley, make sure Jackson doesn't get hurt."

And when his endless tantrums drove them up the wall, *I* would always be the one who had to stop him from screaming, and kicking, and fighting, because I was the only one who could calm him down.

Not that he's like that all the time. There are times when Jackson is so sweet and so loving that he makes you forget how unreasonable he was just five minutes before. And then there are the times he just makes you pull your hair out!

"Jackson, you'd better come out now, or I swear I'll—"

"You're not playing right," said Jackson. "You gotta play right. You gotta look for me."

Outside, lightning struck, bathing the solemn stone heads around me with a cold light that cast their eyes deep in shadow. We were the only ones in the gallery now. All the other tourists had moved on.

"Come fine me, Ashley. You have to!"

"You better hope I don't!" I shouted.

I ducked past a statue of a plumed serpent, around the chiseled face of a Mayan god. Finally I found Jackson standing on a worn stone altar behind a sign that said, DO NOT STAND ON ALTAR in both Spanish and English. His fists were at his waist like the Jolly Green Giant.

"Look at me!" he said. "I'm a Mexican statue!"

"Mom already told you not to climb!" I looked at the Aztec altar and glanced at the placard explaining it. I shivered in spite of myself. "You stand up there, some Aztec might come and cut out your heart—that's what they used it for!"

Jackson paled at the thought. "Did not! You're lying!"

"It says right here. Now let's go!" I pulled him off the altar, and he struggled against my grip.

"No, I wanna stay here. I wanna play hide-and-seek," he said. "And I'm hungry, too. I want a corn dog."

"You can't have one!" I shouted. "You're in Mexico. They don't have corn dogs here."

"You're lying. You're just being mean!" Jackson screamed back at me. He was beyond reason, and I was beyond patience. Mom and Dad were probably halfway through the museum now, and I was getting a headache from Jackson's voice and the city's thin air. So I grabbed him and carried him off, kicking and screaming.

"No! I won't go!" he wailed. "I won't, I won't, I won't!" He bit me on the arm, I dropped him, and he ran—

—right into a dark stone slab.

Jackson bounced off it and fell to the ground. "You did that on purpose!" he insisted. "You pushed me!"

The leash on my temper was fraying, but I held onto it, figuring that maybe now he'd come along calmly. He turned to the figure carved into the stone slab; a young warrior with angry eyes.

"You stink," he told it, still holding the spot on his forehead that had rammed the slab.

"I wouldn't say that to him. Says here that this is Tez-catlipoca—the god of the night wind. It says he could become an angry wind that sweeps unwary travelers away. I wouldn't mess with a guy like that!"

I looked around and noticed that this slab wasn't on a pedestal. In fact, it was right in the middle of an aisle. No wonder Jackson ran into it. I tried to remember if we saw it when we first entered the huge gallery, but for the life of me I could not remember seeing that face before.

"Is he a bad-guy?" asked Jackson.

Lightning struck somewhere far away. The light played off Tezcatlipoca's carved lips. I couldn't tell whether he was smiling, or grimacing.

"No," I told Jackson. "He's just a piece of rock."

"If he's supposed to be so mean," said Jackson, "then how come he winked at me?"

"Don't be silly," I said, and pulled him away.

There are mistakes we make that seem tiny and unimportant at the time—but turn into monster regrets. The kind of regrets that shred your dreams into nightmares over and over again.

What happened next, well, that's *my* monster regret, and no one else's.

I headed out with Jackson to find Mom and Dad, but they weren't in the next gallery, or the one after that. I guess even they got overloaded on the wall-to-wall rocks. We weaved quickly through the maze of dead civilizations: Aztec, Olmec, Toltec, and Mayan. And somewhere along the way, I let go of Jackson's hand.

Finally I rounded a corner to find Mom and Dad studying the features of a fertility statue.

"There you are!" said Mom, not even realizing how far behind we had been. "Where's Jackson?"

"Right here . . ." I said, but when I turned, he wasn't there. "Oh, great!"

"You were supposed to keep an eye on him," chided Dad.

I just boiled at Jackson's continual ability to get me in trouble.

"Jackson, c'mon!" I called. "No hide-and-seek!" I felt dizzy, and a bit off balance. I thought I was light-headed from the altitude, but an instant later I realized the ground was moving.

We were having an earthquake.

It wasn't what I expected an earthquake to feel like. It didn't grind and make lots of noise. Instead, it kind of just sloshed back and forth, like we were standing on Jell-O.

It wasn't big. It didn't last long. And somewhere far away, I heard a deep, heavy *boom!* as something fell.

"Jackson?" called Mom, her worry slowly building.

The tremor was over, and I glanced outside. It was darker, and although the rain had stopped, a night wind blew a flock of twisted papers through the museum's courtyard.

"Jackson, this is not funny!" said Dad in his sternest voice.

Jackson didn't answer.

And suddenly, I knew where he must have gone. He went to take one more look at the stone face of Tezcatlipoca—to see if it really had winked at him.

"Oh no!" I raced back through the winding corridors. Whatever had fallen, it was back that way, and I kept trying to tell myself that Jackson was nowhere near it. We'd find him, Dad would scold him, and we'd go back to our hotel and finish up our vacation.

But we couldn't find him.

Instead, we found a two-ton granite slab that had fallen facedown in the aisle.

The image of Tezcatlipoca.

"Jackson!" screamed Mom. She seemed uncertain whether to be angry or to panic. We all kept believing that he'd leap out from behind some other statue. But he didn't. We had security search the museum for hours, but no Jackson.

Finally, long after closing, they brought a winch to raise the massive stone. We huddled together, Mom, Dad, and I, not wanting to look but knowing we had to. Inch by inch, they raised the slab, until the museum lights lit the space beneath.

And nothing was there.

Nothing but the chiseled face of the slab, and the smiling, scowling image of the god of the night wind.

It's easy to rebuild a house. I know because we had to do it after a hurricane once. But rebuilding a *home*—well, that's something different. Because how can you hope to make a home again, when one of the most important parts is missing?

We never found Jackson. Mom and I stayed in Mexico for weeks, and Dad stayed for months, working with the authorities and chasing blind leads until there was nothing for him to do but come back to Florida and go on with life.

Although my parents never blamed me, I knew it was my fault, and that weight pressed on me like a thousand stone slabs. There were times I would look out from our beach house, across the Gulf of Mexico. I would imagine I could see Jackson still there, hiding behind a giant, fat-cheeked Olmec head. Waiting for us to find him.

We limped along, day to day, for almost a year . . . until the storm.

The news report called it a tropical depression—a slow swirling storm that was riding up the Yucatán Peninsula. Mom and Dad watched the TV with mild disinterest . . . which was the way they looked at everything these days. They had become way too quiet over the months, and surf pounding on the beach sounded almost deafening when we sat together.

"Do you think it'll come this way?" I asked Dad.

"What?"

"You know, the storm." I pointed at the screen, but the weather map was already gone.

I would have forgotten about it . . . but the next day that tropical depression was upgraded to a tropical storm, and the day after that it was a full-fledged hurricane.

Florida has always been like a magnet for hurricanes, so the storm was on everyone's mind at school and throughout the neighborhood. We watched the Weather Channel for days, soaking in the reports, as Hurricane Zelda pummeled Galveston, Texas and continued hugging the Gulf Coast.

"It probably won't come this way," Mom said. But hurricanes don't follow any set path. They wander over ocean and shore until they finally die. No telling where they'll head.

It was the morning after Zelda hit Galveston, that I got my first hint of strange events yet to come. Dad was sitting at the breakfast table, the morning news spread out in front of him like a mask hiding his face from the world. The front page faced me—a full-color picture of the hurricane's devastation.

"Wow!" I said as I studied the picture. "Looks like Zelda shows no mercy." There was nothing left of a beach house but a pile of wet rubble. I'd seen storm damage like that before, but it's still hard to comprehend.

"The news is making too big a deal of it," Dad said. "Actually only a few homes were destroyed." Then he showed me a picture on the page he was reading—the same ruined house, viewed from a distance. There were homes still standing on either side of the wreckage. Sure, they had broken windows and all, but had taken nowhere near the damage that the house in the middle had.

"Probably had termites to begin with," Dad suggested. "A storm can do lots of damage when the wood's weak."

I glanced at the color picture on the front again and this time noticed something curious I hadn't seen before.

The wood of the ruined house was a pale blue, and a gray flap of shredded fabric hung from what used to be a window.

"That house was blue, with gray awnings!" I told my parents. "Just like ours!"

"It's a popular color scheme," explained Mom. And although I wanted to talk more about it, Dad had already turned the page to the sports section.

With winds peaking at 150 miles per hour, Zelda wasted New Orleans.

We watched in numb disbelief as the news showed communities devastated by the raging winds and rain. With the hurricane growing in strength, more homes were washed away by the storm's power. A reporter stood in the ruins of one of the worst piles of wreckage—and although they say seeing is believing, I wasn't ready to believe anything just yet . . . but I was getting close.

"Blue wood and gray awnings," I pointed out to my parents. They had no comment this time. From the look of this waterfront Louisiana community, it seemed to have taken a hard slam from this angry storm. But this blue house seemed to have taken it worse than any other.

"Spooky," I said as I stared at the screen. "Jackson would have said that Zelda's favorite color is blue."

Dad left the room at the mention of Jackson's name, and Mom slipped out afterward . . . but I couldn't leave. I suddenly found my mind fixed on those damage reports, awed by the power of winds that could raise oceans and hurl boats half a mile inland.

There was one boat wedged in the side of a truck. The image made me smile in spite of the destruction, because it reminded me of Jackson and the way he loved to play demolition derby. Especially with trains.

It wasn't until I saw the next report that I began to get a funny feeling inside. Like the kind you get about a minute before you have to throw up.

Three derailed trains.

They were miles inland, but a stray edge of the hurricane seemed to have lashed out and whipped them off their tracks.

My brain told me that it was all coincidence—it had to be. But intuition was filling my arms with gooseflesh and making my heart just about explode out of my chest. *Jackson didn't just disappear,* my inner voice shouted to my disbelieving brain. *He disappeared into thin air.... He disappeared into the wind.*

It was a thought I simply couldn't push away. Instead, it built inside of me, like a hurricane in my own head, until I began to believe it ... more than believe—I *knew*. I knew exactly what had happened to my brother so many months before—and exactly what was happening now!

My parents were already asleep, but I shook them awake. My breathing was shallow, and my eyes must have been panicked because they sat up right away and asked what was wrong.

I didn't know what to tell them. I knew what I was thinking, but how could I explain it? How could I explain that the hurricane wasn't destroying homes that looked like ours by accident. This hurricane was *looking* for something, and when it didn't find what it searched for, the storm tore everything to shreds, like ...

... like a child having a tantrum.

The truth was, Hurricane Zelda wasn't a "Zelda" at all.

It was a "Jackson."

"The hurricane," I told my parents. "I think it's heading this way." We turned the news back on, and the weatherman confirmed what I already knew in my heart. The hurricane had abandoned Louisiana and was cutting a fast, furious path across the gulf, toward the Florida coast.

By dawn, the sea was already climbing the old grass-covered dunes, just behind our back porch. An hour later, they gave the order to evacuate.

No one was ready—no one expected the storm to pick up speed and change its course the way it had. Neighbors frantically nailed plywood over their windows as police urged everyone to leave their homes.

Mom and Dad packed our car with whatever it would hold, and we drove inland toward a Red Cross shelter. I looked out the back window of the car at the dark angry sky looming over the horizon, wondering what the storm would do, and where it would go when it found our house empty.

That's when I realized it *couldn't* find our house empty.

With the wind already whipping the trees around us, we got caught in an evacuation traffic jam. If I was going to do it, I had to do it now. Around me random things were thrown that my parents chose to save. Memories, mostly. One memory poked out of a box beside me—the tattered ear of a gnawed teddy bear. It was Jackson's Nighty Bear. It was missing a leg and oozed white fluff from a dozen moth holes—still, Jackson would never sleep without it.

I grabbed Nighty Bear and opened my door.

"Ashley? Ashley, what are you doing?"

But I didn't answer. Instead I ran into the wind, and toward the approaching storm.

The ocean had already begun to swallow our neighborhood by the time I arrived. Waves washed through streets and alleys, while up above, roofs were shredded by the relentless wind. The hurricane had hit with its full, blind fury, ravaging the town.

I fought the rampage of the winds and waters. Cold and shivering, I held on to Jackson's waterlogged bear. I knew my parents must have been coming after me, but I wouldn't look back, for fear that I might get caught and be pulled away to safety.

With the ocean waist deep around me, an undercurrent pulled my feet out and I went down. I gulped a heavy dose of salty sea before a wave carried me back to the surface, and *bam!* I found myself coughing up water on a tilted porch. A blue porch. I was home!

The house was shifting horribly, and it shuddered every time a wave crashed against it. It had already been washed off its foundation, and it would soon go down completely. Before a wave could wash me away, I climbed in through a broken window and fell to the flooded floor.

The TV and living room furniture were floating, like shipwrecks, half submerged around the crooked room. Another wave came crashing through the kitchen window.

I knew what I was thinking was crazy. I knew that I would probably die—but I had to go through with this. I climbed the crooked stairs toward my brother's room.

Jackson's room had been kept in perfect condition. His cartoon bedspread smooth and neat, his fingerpaints tacked up on the wall. But now the wind and rain poured through his broken window, and the floorboards were beginnning to buckle from the strain on the shifting house.

Okay, I'm here, I told myself. *Now what?*

There was a great gnashing noise, and the roof peeled off like the lid of a can, tumbling upward, until it had shredded to smithereens. Now the only thing above me was a screaming tantrum of violent skies. With both hands, I took the ruined bear and held it high above my head, toward the dark clouds.

"Jackson!" I screamed. I couldn't hear my own voice above the wailing wind. "Jackson, it's Ashley!" The wind ripped Nighty Bear from my hands, and it tumbled straight up until it disappeared. "Jackson, you stop this!" I demanded of the storm. "You come down here now!" The wind changed its pitch; now it sounded like a voice, a frightened, angry voice.

I didn't pretend to understand a force that could turn a child into the wind. I could never understand that kind of power.

But I have some power of my own—because I was the only one who could calm Jackson down. I held out my hands to the sky, swallowing my fear. "I'm here, Jackson!" I called out, and I imagined my voice carrying over the winds and out into the ocean, my words reaching the far edge of the storm. "I'm here . . . and you're home!"

The wind tore at me so strongly that I could barely see. I could feel the clouds collapsing, compressing, squeezing between my outstretched arms until the sound of the storm had changed into the screams and sobs of a child.

What had once been wind tearing at me were now struggling arms and legs—kicking and fighting as I held him in my arms . . . as I held my brother. Soon his struggling weakened, and his screams turned to sobs, and then to whimpers as he clutched me tightly around the neck, gripping his Nighty Bear in his cold hand.

"It's okay, Jackson," I told him softly. "It'll be okay." He dug his face into my shoulder and closed his eyes, relaxing at last. And that is how my parents found me—holding my lost brother and gently rocking him to sleep, to the sound of flood waters washing back to join the sea, in a roofless house, beneath a clear, cloudless sky.

•

I know there will be lots of questions. Many will be left unanswered, and even more left unasked. But that's all right. And even though we stand in the shattered debris of our house, I am not sad at all. Because now that Jackson's back, our home is once again whole. And a house can always be rebuilt.

OPABINIA

••••••••••••••••••••••••••••••••••••••

Darren wouldn't have believed it if he hadn't seen it with his own two eyes—a man, appearing out of nowhere in his room, in the dead of night, stuck halfway into the wall.

It was Darren Strongwater's first mysterious visitor, but not the last.

His father would have called it a dream, and his grandfather would have called it a vision, but Darren knew that it was real—he was awake, and completely alert.

This first night visitor was in a great deal of pain—so much pain that he couldn't even scream. The reason clearly had to do with the way he had materialized, halfway into the wall, his head and shoulders hanging out through the wallpaper like a weird trophy head.

Darren couldn't scream either—the shock of seeing a man, or at least half a man, appear in his room was too much for him. His throat closed up in terror, and he could only watch as the man struggled uselessly to pull himself free. Darren couldn't begin to imagine how incredible the pain must have been—to suddenly have the molecules of your body invaded by the plaster and wood of the wall, and the dense copper plumbing behind it. Even now, Darren could hear the pipes creaking and straining as they tried to share the same space as the man in the wall.

Darren wanted to turn away, but the desperation in the visitor's eyes was more powerful than his own fear. Darren felt drawn toward the dying man, and before he realized what he was doing, Darren's feet were crossing the cold wooden floor toward him.

"B . . . B . . . Bu . . ."

The visitor was trying to say something, but his lungs, invaded by the plasterboard wall, couldn't push out enough air for him to speak. Darren watched in the dim moonlight, close enough to hear, but not close enough to be grabbed by the desperately struggling hands.

Then the visitor locked his eyes on Darren, forced his shallow breath a bit deeper, and hissed out a word.

"B . . . Bu . . . Burgess . . ." he said. "Burgesssss . . ."

And with his last moment of life, the visitor pressed the button on a calculator he was carrying. Suddenly he vanished just as quickly as he had appeared . . . and every pipe in the wall burst.

When the Strongwaters purchased the home, they knew the plumbing was old, but never suspected it would be explosive.

"Never seen anything like this," said the plumber examining the hole. "What did you do, flush some dynamite?"

Of course Darren didn't tell anyone what really happened. His father made it very clear that strange occurrences were not discussed in the Strongwater household. The last time Darren had tried to talk to them about strange happenings, it blew up in his face with more force than the exploding pipes.

It had to do with the voices.

Lately there had been people talking in Darren's head when he least expected it—but in a world where the only voices in one's head usually come from a Walkman, the announcement didn't go over very well.

"Voices? What do you mean voices?" his father had said. "You don't hear voices!" It was as if proclaiming they didn't exist would make the voices go away. But they didn't. They only got louder, sometimes waking Darren out of a deep sleep. He never understood what they said, but he knew they were talking to him. Him and no one else. It made him feel important. It made him feel special.

It made everyone else think he was crazy.

"He's doing it for attention," his father had concluded.

"It's the stress of moving to the city," Mom had decided.

"The boy's a shaman," Grandfather announced, and that killed any hope of discussion—because if there was anything Darren's father despised, it was the traditions that Grandfather held so dear.

So they did the proper, modern thing and sent the boy to a psychologist, who did nothing but listen, which was useless, since Darren refused to talk to her.

And so Darren knew better than to tell his family about last night's visitor, and he didn't need a psychologist to tell him that seeing the visitor pushed things to a new level. Either he was very, very sick, or someone really was trying to communicate with him.

The hole in the wall proved to Darren that he wasn't crazy after all. He just had to figure out who this "Burgess" was.

* * *

The second visitor suffered a fate even crueler than the first. Darren's walk to school through the city streets of Providence took him past a trendy block lined with coffeehouses, cafés, and a microbrewery that manufactured its own brand of beer. Through the plate-glass window, you could see the vats of brewing hops and barley, and every afternoon the place turned into a pub, packed with the business crowd.

At eight in the morning, however, the brewery was quiet as Darren passed by—until a sudden pounding came from inside one of the vats. The one closest to where Darren was passing.

"There's ... there's someone in there!" shouted a worker, and a few minutes later they pulled a limp woman out of the brew. The vat had been sealed—there was no way she could have gotten in. Still, she was there.

Later that day, the news confirmed what Darren had already suspected. No one could identify the dead woman—and the only thing she had with her was a calculator that had shorted out.

That night, after his parents had gone to sleep, Darren went into his grandfather's room and told him about the woman. The old man listened patiently as Darren recounted the story.

"I have the strongest feeling that she came from somewhere else," Darren told his grandfather. "That she came to speak to *me*—but she failed."

He thought his grandfather might come up with some powerful words of ancient wisdom to explain the cruelness of this woman's fate, and her mystical appearance. But instead the old man just looked away wearily and said, "I think, maybe, your parents are right. And maybe it's best if you tell this to your psychologist friend."

After that, Darren decided he had to ignore the voices and

the visitors if he was ever going to lead a normal life. He would deny their existence; choose not to see or hear them.

But as it turned out, he had little choice in the matter.

"Don't be afraid."

The third visitor didn't appear in the wall, or in a vat of beer. Instead he appeared at the mall, sitting across from Darren in the food court.

A few feet away, a little girl in a ketchup-stained dress tugged at her mother's sleeve, pointing to the man who had just appeared out of midair, but other than that, no one noticed the sudden appearance—they were too involved in conversations and shoveling down lunch.

Darren wanted to scream long and loud, until mall security arrived to take this invader away, but he didn't. Who would believe him? This visitor seemed just like anyone else in the mall, from his jeans to the backpack he carried. So instead of screaming, Darren filled his mouth with his frozen yogurt until the urge to scream had been numbed.

"I don't want to frighten you," the visitor began. "I don't want to hurt you . . . but we need your help."

Darren studied the man's face. He had a strange tan, and features that seemed to be an exotic mix of many backgrounds. Darren knew about that. Although his father was Manahonset Indian, his mother was half Irish, half Polish—so Darren ended up looking like a red-headed, pale-skinned Manahonset. But this dark-skinned, light-haired man seemed even more a mix than himself. Even his eyes were a speckled hazel—not blue, green, or brown. Darren forced himself to look into the visitor's eyes, hoping to find something—proof of his intentions, maybe. Proof that he was honest, or proof that he was lying, but nothing about the visitor's eyes gave anything away.

Darren didn't know whether he was safe or in grave, grave danger.

"My grandfather believes that ancient spirits can visit us," said Darren. "But I'm not sure I do."

"It doesn't matter either way," said the man. "Because I'm not an ancient spirit." He brushed some crumbs off the table in front of him, as if the very presence of dirt offended him. "My name is Rance," he said. "I come from the distant future—a time called the Age of Understanding. We've been trying to contact you for quite a while—you've heard us, no doubt."

Darren nodded. "Seen you, too." He curled his toes in his shoes, determined not to show his fear. "So if you're from the Age of Understanding," asked Darren, "how come the people you send, appear in walls, and get themselves drowned? Sounds like you don't understand much about time travel."

Rance stiffened just a bit at the mention of it. "If you understood the nature of time as well as we do, then you'd know that time travel is imperfect," he answered. "Time is constantly moving—slithering, like a snake with its head and tail gripping the end of infinity."

"Really," said Darren with a grin. "I always thought time was like a snake swallowing its own tail."

Rance was not amused.

"Time travel is not something to be taken lightly," he said. "In fact, we've come to understand that time travel should be avoided at all costs."

"Then why are you here?" Darren dared to ask. "And why are you bothering me?"

Rance smiled, showing his perfect teeth, white as polished ivory. "Because, young man, we need you for a mission of great importance. You, and no one else."

Darren's heart, as fast as it pounded, picked up the pace.

"You need me to come into the future?" Darren asked, not knowing whether he was more excited or frightened.

"No," answered Rance. "Not quite." Rance leaned in closer and lowered his voice to a whisper. "Have you ever heard of the Burgess Shale?"

Darren shook his head. "No."

Then Rance pulled out a small white stone from his pocket and dropped it into Darren's hand. As Darren examined it closely, he realized it wasn't a stone at all, but a tooth. A sharp, barbed tooth.

"The Burgess Shale," repeated Rance. "I suggest you learn about it." Then he vanished as quickly as he had come, and at the next table, the ketchup-stained girl tugged on her mother's sleeve again.

Burgess Shale, the encyclopedia entry read. *Only ten feet high, and a city block long, the Burgess Shale is one of the most important discoveries of prehistoric fossils ever unearthed.*

Aside from his collection of plastic dinosaurs, Darren knew painfully little about the distant past. Until now, he had never realized it could be of any importance to him. Apparently the Burgess Shale was discovered nearly a hundred years ago somewhere up in Canada. It held no dinosaur bones, however—these fossils came from a time millions of years before the dinosaurs, when life teemed in hot seas that covered most of the globe. Three hundred and fifty million years ago, to be exact.

Caught in a massive prehistoric mudslide, the fossils of the Burgess Shale are almost perfectly preserved, continued the encyclopedia, *and give us a clear view of the late Cambrian period.*

Darren turned the page to see the bizarre collection of creatures unearthed in the shale; the anomalocaris—a frightening beast with a round, tooth-filled mouth. The hallucigenia—a tiny multilegged thing that seemed so strange to the man who discovered it that he was convinced he was hallucinating.

But nothing could have prepared him for the sight of the opabinia!

It was spectacular, and like nothing Darren had ever imagined. Only three inches long, the unearthly creature had rows of gills running down the sides of its body, a single clawed arm growing from its head, and five eyes that gave it sight in every direction at once. It was weird, and wonderful.

No creature found in the Burgess Shale survives today. In fact, there is nothing even related to these creatures anywhere in the world. The end of the Cambrian period is marked by their mysterious extinction.

Extinction. Now *that* was something Darren knew about. He only had to look in his grandfather's fading eyes to see the extinction of his tribe. His grandfather would tell stories of the Manahonset Indians, and their proud heritage, but fewer and fewer Manahonset remained each year. Like Darren's father, they moved away and abandoned their culture. And so, while other Native American nations thrived, the Manahonset died a little more each day.

In recent years, we've come to realize that these creatures are unique, and unlike anything else that ever lived.

Darren reached into his pocket and pulled out the strange hooked tooth Rance had given him. Instinctively he knew that this was the tooth from the garbage-disposal mouth of anomalocaris!

The great extinction uncovered in the Burgess Shale changed forever the course of evolution, in ways impossible to comprehend.

Darren gripped the tooth tightly in his hand, wondering what all this had to do with him.

* * *

The time traveler next appeared in a phone booth as Darren walked to school the next day. They took the long way, speaking of things wonderfully complex and incomprehensible. Rance bragged about his great knowledge and dazzled Darren with talk of temporal fractals, dimensional loops, and quantum-multiplistic theory.

"We have come to understand that there are eighteen distinct focal points in Earth's history," explained Rance. "Some of them are prehistoric and others more recent—but put together, these eighteen events have determined the course of life, and of mankind."

"What are they?" asked Darren, hungry to know the great answers of the universe, uncovered in the Age of Understanding.

But Rance shook his head. "Not for you to know. . . . But I can tell you this—the event that created the Burgess Shale 350 million years ago is one of the most important events of all. It's also different."

"What makes it so different?"

"Because unlike any other prehistoric event," explained Rance, "our sub-molecular analysis of the Burgess Shale indicates that there was conspicuous human intervention."

Darren wrinkled his brow in confusion. "What do you mean?"

"I mean that at the time of the great Cambrian extinction . . . *people were there*. Two people, to be exact."

"People? But . . . but how?" asked Darren. "People weren't around for millions of years. . . ."

Rance produced a small calculator from his backpack—just like the one the first two unlucky time travellers had carried. "This is how."

Darren looked at it closely to see that the calculator had a glowing green button, dead center.

"It has taken hundreds of years to generate enough energy to power a 350-million-year time-transport."

"To the Cambrian period!" Darren shouted. "To see what really happened!"

"You're catching on!" said Rance, placing the time-calculator-thingy in Darren's hands. "This is yours. I have my own."

"Wait—You mean—"

"I mean that *you* are to accompany me to the distant past. You will be witness to one of the most important events in prehistory."

Darren held the device as if it were a tiny nuclear bomb. "Why me?" he asked.

Rance laughed as if the question was stupid and the answer obvious.

"Because in our infinite understanding," explained the arrogant time traveler, "we have concluded that of all the humans who have ever lived, *you* are the one who must go."

Darren let his words echo deep within his soul. He had always felt he was meant for something special in the great design of things. Perhaps his destiny truly was a great one! But still, there was a part of him that wanted to know more— *needed* to know more. And he was afraid.

"Wh—what if I don't want to go?"

Rance smiled in that superior way of his. "Oh, you'll go," he said. "History shows that you *did* go, and if there's one thing we know, it's that history doesn't change."

"But—"

Rance dismissed Darren's questioning with a wave of his hand. It made Darren furious. Just because he was from the Age of Understanding didn't give Rance the right to treat Darren this way.

"Whether it's today, or whether it's tomorrow, you're going

to hit that button," Rance proclaimed. "And when you do, I'll be waiting for you there, at the edge of the prehistoric sea."

Rance did not come again. Not that night, nor the next day, nor the day after that. Darren wanted Rance to return and plead with Darren to press the button. How could Rance be so arrogant—so sure that Darren would go. But Darren knew the answer.

Because I've already gone.

Somehow, they know the past. They *understand* the past, and if it already happened, Rance is right—Darren would press that button someday and transport to that impossibly distant point in history, when the opabinia, the anomalocaris, and many other strange creatures swam the seas.

What made it worse was that Darren really *did* want to go. It was a grand destiny indeed to be chosen to witness one of the most important events since the beginning of time—but what good was such a destiny if he had no choice in it? Being chosen can only be special when you have the choice to refuse. Without that choice, he was merely a tiny gear in the machinery of the universe. Machinery he could never change.

So he refused to push the button.

He refused for a whole month. He barely ate, he barely spoke. His parents, more worried than ever, sent him on extra visits to the psychologist.

Then came the dream. It came on a night when the wind howled and sounded alive with mournful wails. In his dream Darren was trapped in the Burgess Shale, buried beneath tons of mud that had hardened into rock over millions of years. And in the stone around him, a million creatures called out his name. *"Darren ... Darren,"* they cried. *"Come to us ... join us,"* they wailed. *"You can't change what has already been. ..."* A school of one-clawed opabinia swarmed around him, moving through the stone, their five unblinking eyes staring at him. He tried to scream, but his mouth was filled with stone. He had no flesh—only bone. *He* was the fossil now . . . but he wasn't the only one. Beside him was his father, and then his grandfather, and then his great-grandfather. The shale was filled with the bones of the Manahonset, their ancient voices silenced by the stone.

Darren awoke in a cold sweat, gasping for breath, still feeling the heavy pressure of the shale all around him.

Finally the dream faded away, but the images remained in his mind. And that's when he knew he had to go.

He had to see the opabinia—because he understood what it meant to be lost when the world changed. As he lay there in bed, Darren could hear his grandfather snoring weakly in the next room. His grandfather no longer told the old stories like he used to, and when he died, he would take with him a history that should have been Darren's. That was an end just as final as the opabinia's.

So he finally took the time-calculator and punched the button. Not because Rance said he would, but because the opabinia deserved the dignity of a witness. Someone to affirm its life and tell its tale. Someone to make it matter.

The moment he pressed the button, an intense pain shot through him. It was like being turned inside out, while being fired from a cannon, while boiling in acid. He saw time peel away before him, the days spinning like a strobe light until the sun and moon were streaks in the sky. But he wasn't only moving through time, he was moving through space as well, rocketing through solid mountains, moving north, toward the great Burgess Shale.

It seemed to last an eternity, and yet it was over before Darren drew a single breath—and when he did, the air was hot and thick with sulfur, like the smell of a million rotten eggs. The sky was red instead of blue and the air so humid he felt he could almost swim in it.

"There you are," he heard a familiar voice next to him say.

"Waiting long?" Darren sneered.

"Six minutes," said Rance. "Your machine was programmed to bring you here five minutes after I arrived—but, as I said, time travel is imperfect."

Darren looked out over the vista in front of him, and if there had been any anger, any frustration in him, it was washed away by the magnificent sight of Cambrian Earth.

Before him was a great inland sea, surrounded by cliffs hundreds of feet high. It was near sunset, and in the fading light, creatures left phosphorescent trails like underwater fireworks stretching as far as the eye could see.

Darren could only stare in amazement.

"I know," said Rance. "No one has ever seen such splendor, nor will anyone ever see it again."

"Can I get closer?"

Rance nodded. "You can, and you must," was all he said.

Darren approached the water's edge, and there, wallowing in a tide pool, he saw them for the first time. Opabinia. They were only a few inches long, but breathtaking all the same.

Darren scooped one up, and it wriggled in his hand. Its exoskeleton was not a dull gray armor, but a smooth multicolored shell, reflecting every color of the rainbow. Its five eyes were not empty and cold, but innocent and warm. The claw that grew from its head was not spiny and rough, but soft and velvety.

The creature was not a monster, but a wonder.

"Take a good look," said Rance. "*Your* scientists don't know it—but this is the last place in Cambrian Earth that these creatures still exist." Then he pointed to the enormous cliff that overhung the great inland sea. "In half an hour, that mountain-side will come crashing down, clogging this sea with poisonous mud. Everything in it will die."

Darren gaped at Rance as he finally realized why this moment in time was so important. The mudslide that created the Burgess Shale didn't just capture a sample of these strange creatures—*it snuffed out their very existence!* In half an hour, the opabinia, and countless other creatures, would become extinct!

Darren petted the back of the tiny opabinia. *How unfair,* he thought, *that something so wondrous had to die off.*

He was still thinking of the doomed opabinia when Rance grabbed his hand. By the time Darren heard the clink of metal, it was too late. He looked down to see his arm handcuffed to a chain and the chain locked to a steel spike that was embedded in the stone beneath them.

"Wh—what's this?" Darren asked lamely.

"History in the making," answered Rance, just as calmly as could be. "Do you remember that tooth I gave you? That tooth belonged to quite a large anomalocaris. While your scientists were only able to take the fossil and reconstruct what the creature looked like, we, in the Age of Understanding, were able to uncover its entire genetic structure . . . and do you know what we found?"

Darren tugged at his chain. It clanked in the thick sulfuric air, but held him tight.

"We found two very distinct chains of DNA," continued Rance. "One belonged to the anomalocaris itself, and the other belonged to *the last thing the anomalocaris ate.*"

Even in the hot air of the Cambrian dusk, Darren felt a chill rocket up his highly evolved spine. "Me?"

"You," answered Rance. "No one else in the universe has your exact DNA. It took us many years to track you down, and many months trying to contact you, but ultimately we knew we would."

Darren screamed in furious terror: *"You brought me here to be eaten?"*

"Be proud," said Rance calmly. "Very few people know their purpose in the universe."

There was a sound in the sea behind him, like a groan coming up from deep in the shimmering water. The clanking of his chains had drawn the attention of something beneath the waters.

"No!" screamed Darren. "I won't let it happen!"

"No sense fighting it," said Rance. "It already did happen. It's just a matter of letting the event play through to its natural conclusion."

Still, Darren tugged on his chains. To die was bad enough; to be eaten was even worse. But to be eaten by something that would itself die in half an hour—Darren could not imagine a more meaningless end.

"So the only reason you came here was to feed me to this . . . to this *thing*?"

"No," said Rance. "I also came to detonate this." He reached into his backpack—the one he always carried—and pulled out a bulky device with wires and a clock. Even in the Age of Understanding, a bomb looked like a bomb.

All at once Darren realized the full extent of Rance's mission. "You're going to start the mudslide that kills off all of these creatures, aren't you!"

"That is *my* purpose," answered Rance, "to prune the tree of evolution, and make sure that these creatures die, paving the way for life as we know it."

With his free hand, Darren reached for his time-travel device and punched the button. But nothing happened. In fact, the dim digital readout died completely.

"Your transporter only had enough power for a one-way trip," explained Rance. "We, in the Age of Understanding, believe in conserving energy when we can."

And with that, Rance turned and headed up toward the cliff with his bomb of extinction.

The water began to ripple around Darren's feet, and the school of opabinia wallowing in the tide pool flung themselves back into the sea, in a race to escape what was approaching.

A pearly white glow rose to the surface.

"No!" screamed Darren *"No!"*

The anomalocaris launched itself out of the water and into the tide pool. It was only two feet long, but as deadly as something ten times its size, with sharp, gleaming pincers. It came at Darren, its circular, tooth-filled mouth ready to eat this new-found futuristic delight. Darren kicked it away with his foot, but it slithered back toward him again in the shallow water. Then a second one surfaced and launched toward him. And then a third.

"I will not die this way!" Darren insisted. He knew his will to live flew in the face of history, but still he fought his destiny with everything he had.

Over and over the prehistoric beasts attacked—but they had not evolved intelligence—they couldn't learn from their mistakes. Each time the beasts launched the exact same attack, and each time, Darren was able to kick them away with his foot . . . but one slip and Darren's foot would be caught in one of their deadly mouths, and that would be his end.

If he could break free from his chain, he could still run away. He could make it out of the ravine before Rance detonated his bomb of extinction. Even if history said he didn't escape, he had to try.

When the next anomalocaris attacked, Darren plunged his hand deep into its mouth, gagging it, and then pulled his hand out quickly. The dumb beast bit down, missing his hand, but caught the chain—

—and the force of its bite split the chain in two!

Darren kicked it away for the last time, scrambled out of the tide pool, and raced up the steep slope, following the footprints of Rance . . . while behind him the three anomalocari slipped back into the sea, in search of other prey.

Rance had been so sure of himself. They thought they had all the answers in the Age of Understanding—but they didn't, did they? For Darren had changed his own destiny. He had altered the course of history and would not end up in the bellies of the doomed beasts. His DNA would never end up on that tooth! Even as he climbed the mountain he could feel the change radiating forward from this moment, toward infinity— the great serpent of time writhing in agony as all of eternity adjusted itself. It was a feeling of enormous power.

At the top of the ridge Darren came across Rance, kneeling over his bomb. He wasn't expecting to see Darren again, and when he did, the color drained from his face. It was wonderful to see the Man of Understanding at a loss for words.

"But . . . but you can't be here! It's impossible."

"Sorry," said Darren, "but we, in the Age of Video, don't believe anything's impossible."

Darren ran forward and kicked the bomb away from Rance.

"No!" Rance screamed, "you don't know what you're doing. This bomb *must* go off! The mudslide won't happen without it!"

Now Darren was the one who could afford to be smug. "Maybe it's just me, but I don't believe in killing off endangered species—even ones that lived 350 million years before I was born!"

Darren grinned and tore the wires from the bomb. It had no backup triggers because the Wise Ones hadn't expected anyone would tamper with it. And so when Darren pulled its wires, its timer stopped dead.

Rance, his eyes wide in disbelief, backed away from Darren in terror. "It *will* go off!" Rance screamed. "It has to go off! You can't change what's already happened. You can't ch—"

And then the time traveler took one step too far, lost his balance, and tumbled off the prehistoric cliff.

Darren leapt forward, trying to catch him, but it was too late. He could only watch as the Man of Understanding tumbled a thousand feet into the great inland sea. There was a thrashing of white water, and his body was gone—devoured by a school of anomalocari—perhaps the same ones that were meant to eat Darren.

Feeling weak from the thinness of the oxygen and the terror of the moment, Darren fell to his knees and found himself staring at the defused bomb. But that didn't interest him. What interested him was the small calculator-like device beside it. Rance had dropped his time-transporter, and *this* one had the power for a return trip!

Darren took the defused bomb and hurled it off the cliff, so it could do no harm. Then he programmed a date and time into the calculator and punched the green button.

Intense pain turned him inside out as he shot forward to the distant future, and home.

His parents found him lying on the bathroom floor, his hand gripping his gut in pain. The trip home had been far worse than his trip to the Cambrian sea. It was as if his body had been shredded, reformed, and shredded again. He could barely move. But at least he hadn't materialized in a solid wall.

"Darren! Darren, honey," wailed his mom. "Are you all right?"

Darren took a deep breath, and another, and another. The

pain was quickly subsiding. "It was a dream," he told them. "Just a bad dream." Although he knew it was real.

His grandfather went to get him a drink, and his father helped him up. "C'mon, Darren, it's only a dream. Everyone has nightmares."

They helped him back to bed, and once everyone had left his room, Darren tried to replay what he had seen—what he had lived through—but the images were already getting lost in confusion. He couldn't even remember what Rance looked like.

Rance had been so afraid of Darren's changing a key event in history—but after all his worries, had anything really changed? For an instant Darren thought something might be different, but the feeling washed away with the memory of Rance's face. No, the time traveler had been wrong. Nothing had changed. Everything seemed fine. Everything seemed normal.

And that was good.

Darren fell asleep thinking of the great prehistoric sea. What an amazing sight it was! He wouldn't have believed it if he hadn't seen it with his own five eyes.

DAWN
TERMINATOR

•••

We lost contact with Denver at 4:00 A.M.

That's what the newswoman says on TV. Her hair's a ragged mess, and her hands fidget in desperation—the kind of desperation news anchors aren't supposed to show.

I'm cold and frightened. Terrified of the night outside the huge airport windows and terrified of the noisy crowds moving in that darkness. I hate the dark—I hate the night. I've always been a day person—but that doesn't mean much anymore, according to the woman on the news.

In the crowded airport lounge, people stare blankly at the TV screen. A man curses beneath his breath, even as he rocks his baby in his arms. A woman gapes at the screen as she picks nervously at her peeling cuticles. None of these people can stretch their mind around what's happening. I can't either. It's too big—too awful.

So instead of thinking about it, I take a pencil and my sketch pad from my shoulder bag, figuring I'll find something to draw. The man with the baby. The woman tearing at her own fingertips. I always get an intense craving to draw when things around me get too rough to handle. Funny, the things you feel like doing when everything's coming down around you.

Mom reaches over and gently restrains my hand before I can lay pencil to paper.

"No, Lauren, not now."

Dad grabs my younger brother tightly. "We can't stay here, we have to move," Dad says. I look out of the lounge; a heavy current of panicked people flows by, heading toward the gates. I try to see their faces, but they wash by too quickly for me to get an image I can hold. They won't slow down, because they know time is ticking away, and time has become everyone's worst enemy.

My family, like many other people, has stopped in the terminal lounge to rest and catch their breath, but wasting any more time here will be a mistake. There are a thousand—maybe a million other people crammed into the gates and hallways of San Francisco International Airport. We don't have any plane tickets, but then no one does.

"We'll get on a plane," Dad promises as we prepare to force our way into the moving crowd. "We'll make it." Dad's the kind of guy who always manages to get his way, but this is the only time it really matters.

"What will happen when the sun rises?" my brother, Kenny, asks.

"You don't have to worry about that," answers Mom. "We're never going to see the sun rise."

I look at my watch. Forty-three minutes and twenty seconds until dawn. I guess we've all memorized the exact time morning will show its blinding face today. I start to imagine what will happen the moment the sun rises, but my mind shuts off like a circuit breaker—as if just imagining it will burn my mind to a cinder.

No one believed it could happen.

The scientists said it wouldn't—they swore that the warning signs were false and that only lunatics and crackpots would suggest such a thing. The truth is, they didn't want to believe that the Sun could go nova.

But two minutes before midnight, it did.

At 11:58 P.M., Pacific standard time, the sun detonated with a force too immense to calculate—just like the crackpots said it would. Six minutes later, Europe, Asia, Africa—everything east of the Atlantic was gone. There was no one left to tell this half of the world what was waiting for us at dawn ... but we knew.

We knew because of the way transatlantic phone calls suddenly went dead.

We knew because of how brightly the moon suddenly shone in the sky—so bright you couldn't even look at it.

But for our family, it was the honking of horns that woke us up to the truth. Thousands of blaring car horns, all blending together into a panicked siren, loud enough to wake the dead. Every road, every freeway was instantly jammed. We quickly joined in that honking madness, riding over sidewalks and yards, because the roads themselves were already clotted with abandoned cars. I made Dad drive with the dome light on, so Kenny and I wouldn't have to sit in that awfully dark backseat—which seemed worse than any dark I could remember.

In our race to the airport, we passed hordes of people looking heavenward, praying in the streets. I prayed, too. Prayed that we would all be saved—that the earth would stop spinning and that the line of dawn would stop burning its way across the world.

The Terminator—that's what they call the line that divides the night from the day. It stretches from pole to pole, and never stops moving as the earth spins.

But it doesn't *quite* stretch from pole to pole. Far to the north, there are places where the northern lights dance, and the night lasts for months on end. Places beyond the Arctic Circle. It's late November now—that means the sun won't rise there for at least three months. That's where we must go to escape the killing breath of the sun.

And we have forty-one minutes left to fly from the dawn.

As we try to force our way out of the lounge, more people press in. I see a kid I recognize, but he doesn't spare a thought for me—he's trying too hard to catch his breath. In front of us, the mob races past like a rain-swollen river. You can drown in a current like that. I imagine myself pulled down and suffocated beneath the feet of the moving mass. There are so many bodies that they block the fluorescent light from above—it must be pitch black down by the scuffling feet of the crowd. That's a darkness worth being afraid of.

Mom and Dad hold Kenny's and my hands tightly, and we leap into the dangerous crowd.

Instantly we are pulled into the current. I'm whipped in the face by the red-painted nails of a passing hand. A fat man's belt buckle scratches across my side. My bag slips from my shoulder, and although I reach back for it, Mom tugs me along.

"Forget it," she says. "It doesn't matter."

My bag is trampled, and swallowed, disappearing into the darkness. My sketch pad, with all my drawings, is lost—it was the only thing I had wanted to take with me. The faces I had drawn.

Then my hand slips from my mother's.

"Lauren? Lauren!" I hear her call but can't see her.

"Lauren!" Her cries seem farther away, and all I can see are the dark textures of heavy clothes moving all around me. I'm surrounded by people, and yet alone in the crushing crowd. Although I want to scream, I know that giving in to panic will be even more dangerous than being separated from my family. So I bite my fear back and give my will over to the will of the moving mob. Pressed between the crying old woman to my right and the angry bearded man on my left, I let the mob carry me down the endless airport corridor, toward unseen gates of departure.

Gates 44, 45, 46. I see the signs pass by above me—but each gate is mobbed with people—I can't even see if there are planes at the ends of the jetways. Suddenly there's a burst of cold air, as the human river bursts out through an emergency exit. My feet stumble down a set of metal steps, until I set foot on hard asphalt.

The airport tarmac is a huge expanse of concrete covered with airplanes all facing at strange angles. Not normal airport order. I wonder if anyone is even in the air-traffic tower.

There are people everywhere, racing in random directions. A woman with a raging knot of tangled hair uses her suitcase as a battering ram to get past, and she bounces me to the ground.

And there, through the forests of legs, I see a pair of cartoon-character Nikes I recognize—and they're moving away.

But in the last few minutes I've learned some tricks of survival. I force myself forward, slamming my shoulders into legs around me, hitting people, tripping people—everything short of biting them to get them out of my way—until I finally reach out and grab that small foot with both hands.

Kenny screams and looks down.

"It's Lauren!" he cries. "I found Lauren!"

Dad pulls me into his arms. "Thank god! We thought we lost you!"

He and Mom hug me tightly, but only for an instant. There will be time for hugs later, if there's any time at all. I dare to look at my watch. Thirty-four minutes.

The crowds around us are thickest near the planes, where roll-away staircases are blocked by armed security guards. I guess airport security has taken it upon themselves to pick and choose who gets to go on the planes, and it makes me angry— what gives *them* the right to make the choice?

Dad pulls us toward a plane where a guard who couldn't be any older than eighteen bars the way, letting no one up to the hatch. He scans the crowd with wide, anxious eyes as if searching for someone.

We force our way forward until reaching the guard.

"Back off!" yells the guard. "This plane is full." He aims his weapon at my father's chest. Dad ignores the gun.

"I don't think you want to shoot me," Dad warns the guard. "I'm a pilot."

The guard's eyes light up with relief. "From the airline?" he asks.

"Does it matter?" my father answers.

The fact is, my father once flew fighter jets in the air force, and although he hasn't flown for ten years, he's the best hope for this plane. It's now I realize that there aren't enough pilots to fly all these planes.

"Only you can come," the guard tells my father sternly. "No room for the others."

But Dad stands his ground. "Let my family on, or fly the plane yourself."

"There'll be other pilots," the guard insists.

Dad glances at his watch. "Maybe, maybe not," he says. "All I know is that sunrise is less than a half an hour away."

The guard doesn't need any more coaxing. He nods, and we

clatter up the stairs toward the plane. The guard follows right behind us.

At the top of the stairs, I turn to see the mob forcing its way up the stairs. Their pleading cries rise above the rest of the crowd.

"Out of the way!" bellows the guard. He pushes me into the DC-10 and swings the heavy door closed behind us.

Hands pound on the door outside, and through the tiny window in the door I see a man, his face pressed up against the glass by the mob pushing behind him.

I turn away, but Mom gently touches my shoulder.

"No," she says. "Look at them. Study their faces. *Memorize* their faces."

I look at her, confused. "Why?"

"Because your memory of them is all they have left."

And so I do as she says. I make my way through the crowded aisles, force my way to a window seat. Then I peer out the window, at the faces outside.

There are people on the wing now, and more climbing up the engine, to the wing. They pound on the hull until it sounds like a hailstorm. Men, women, children. They pull at the wing flaps in a mad frenzy. I study their faces. I give them names. Mr. Smith. Mrs. Josephs. Bobby, Angela, JJ.

I hear the engines start, and we begin to move forward.

The crowd moves away from the plane—even the maddened people on the wings jump down. Maybe they know that our hope is more important than their desperation.

Then, as we turn to get in line behind a dozen other jets waiting for takeoff, I see the first trace of the coming dawn.

The eastern edge of the sky doesn't shine a faint blue—instead it burns a searing, lethal white, fading into the darkness of the night cover still protecting us. It's just a hint of the dawn soon to come. A warning.

"We have to take off!" people around me shout. "We have to leave now.".

I squirm out into the aisle and over a dozen people until reaching the cockpit where my father mans the controls. He has no co-pilot—only Kenny sits there, kicking his feet. Mom sits in the navigator's seat, trying to make sense of the navigational charts.

I watch the planes before us, taking off one right behind another.

"C'mon, c'mon," my father says, gripping the controls with white knuckles as the eastern sky begins to burn a brighter white.

At last the plane before us accelerates down the runway, and Dad instantly powers our engines to full throttle, right on the other jet's tail—a dangerous but necessary move. I hold on tight as we pick up speed. I feel the front wheels leave the ground, and then the rear. We are airborne!

Dad instantly banks away from the plane just ahead of us, and soon we are heading northwest. I can feel our airspeed as it increases.

We're airborne, but I don't know how safe we are. The minutes fly by much too quickly, and twelve minutes after takeoff we punch through the highest layer of clouds. I dare to look out a side window as we take a sharp bank to avoid another plane.

That's when I see it happen.

The first true rays of sun assault the horizon . . . and the clouds boil away before it, until they are gone.

Far away, at the edge of the horizon, the towers of San Francisco burst into flames—and I swear I see the Golden Gate bridge melt into the bay.

The tiny dots of planes just minutes behind us turn into

fireballs, and Mom gently puts a hand to my face, guiding my eyes away from the window.

"Now's the time to stop looking," says Mom.

I wonder how long it will be until we become like those ill-fated people, disintegrating into the new day. Surely our plane was built to withstand extreme heat and cold. But I don't think its designers had this particular trip in mind.

Inside the cabin, the air temperature keeps rising, but Dad banks us due west and somehow finds even greater airspeed. I turn to him. "Can we make it?" I ask. "Can we outrun the dawn?"

"This is a fast jet," he answers. "We'll see."

In less than a minute that glimmer of sun is gone as we surpass the speed of the spinning earth. The sun seems to set behind us while we keep our eyes locked forward into the trailing edge of night.

12:00 noon. At least that's what my watch says, but time doesn't mean much anymore. It's still dark. We've been spiraling to the north for seven hours, and although the Dawn Terminator is still on the horizon behind us, just as white hot as ever, it's slipping to the south, instead of east. We have already crossed into the Arctic Circle, and Dad banks the plane to the right. Soon we will cross directly over the North Pole ice pack, heading toward a place where the sun won't rise for months.

"What if we can't find a place to land?" Kenny asks, but no one answers him. There's no room anymore for "what ifs."

I leave Dad to worry about that and try to soothe myself by drawing on the back of American Airlines cocktail napkins. I've finished about five of them now and start on a new one.

"What are you drawing?" Mom asks. I show her the napkin

I just finished. They say I have a talent for portraits, and now I have a real reason to draw them.

"Who is it?" Mom asks.

"A woman I saw in the crowd," I tell her. Then I hand her the stack of finished ones. "They're all people I saw in the crowd before we took off."

Mom looks at me with surprise and wonder, and hands me better paper.

"I think we've arrived," says Dad, almost an hour later.

We are over the northern tip of Greenland—Cape Morris Jessup, to be exact. It's the northernmost piece of land on the globe. The glow from the fiery Terminator is far away now. That distant white glow will circle around the North Pole, threatening the horizon for months, until it finally engulfs the entire Arctic Circle. Then this icy land will pay dearly for its many months of darkness—for in the summer months, the midnight sun will burn, and this place will not see night until the fall.

"If the sun won't rise for three months," asks Kenny, "what happens *after* three months?"

Mom and Dad look at each other, unsure how to answer. But I know what the answer is. "We have three months to figure that out," I tell him.

He nods. "That's a long time," he says. I suppose to him it is.

"It'll be long enough," I answer.

My father seems to sit up straighter as he hears me say it. "Yes . . . yes, I think it will be." I can almost see his faith in our survival growing with each second—my mother's, too, as if my hope was a seed for theirs to grow on.

The blue glow of a blinding bright moon paints a landscape of ice beneath us. I'd call it uninviting, but here and now, there's no place on earth I'd rather be. It's bright enough to land on—and bright enough to see a hundred other planes dotting the endless expanse of ice. We weren't the only ones who made it—although we are probably among the last.

Then I feel the plane begin its final descent. With that descent, I can hear voices in the cabin chiming forth offerings of hope.

"I'm a thermal engineer," calls out one man. "I can design heat shields, like the ones they use on the space shuttle."

"Hey," shouts one woman, "what if we fly by night to the South Pole in the summer?"

"Hey," shouts another, "what if we find caverns to give us shelter in the spring and fall?"

"Yeah—we can cultivate crops that grow in darkness. Mushrooms, maybe!"

On and on, until the world we've lost doesn't seem to matter anymore—all that matters is tomorrow, and the next day, and the next.

As I think of it, all at once I feel a rush of heated emotions rising in me with more power than the nova we once called the sun. I feel everything all at once. Anger, fear, sorrow, but also an incredible comfort, and intense joy. Now I realize that this great and awesome cosmic event is not an ending—but it's not really a beginning either; it's a link between what was and what will be. *We* are that link. Mom, Dad, Kenny, and me, and everyone on every plane that made it this far. What a wonderful destiny to be a bridge to the future.

Tears cloud my eyes, and Mom puts an arm around me. "It'll be all right," she says. "You'll see." She thinks my tears are tears of sadness, but they're not—not anymore. Because now I know we'll survive just as surely as I know the sun won't rise. With time finally on our side, we *will* find those safe caverns. We *will* build those heat shields. And when the angry sun does find us after the long night, it will find us ready.

We will adapt. I will adapt.

Our wheels touch the surface of the great expanse of ice, and as I look out the window, I have to smile through my tears. I've already learned to love the night.

MIDNIGHT MICHELANGELO

• •

With the sounds of traffic far below and the dark sky above, fourteen-year-old Mickey Blake hung suspended between the sky and the angry city. He didn't think about how high he was; he thought only about the task at hand: his masterpiece.

Silver paint hissed out the tip of a spray can, leaving a dazzling streak glistening on the metal surface. *Just a few minutes more,* Mickey told himself. *Just a few minutes more and I'll be done.* He had to remind himself not to look down, or he might lose his balance and fall in front of the cars that shot down the freeway. His work on the overpass was almost done . . . just a few finishing touches.

"Mickey!" shouted a voice from below. "Mickey, we've gotta get out of here!" It was Wendy. He could hear the panic in her voice, but figured it was probably nothing major. She simply wasn't used to this sort of thing. But an instant later, Mickey heard the sirens.

"Mickey, hurry!" Wendy shouted. "They're coming!"

"One sec!" he shouted back. "Just one second more." He couldn't stop when he was this close. He had to risk it. Blue and red lights began to play off the colorful work of art in front of him. He clipped the can of silver spray paint onto his mountain-climbing harness and grabbed the blue paint can. Quickly he filled in the blue iris of an eye that was two feet high. Below him he heard the slamming of a car door.

"That's enough, Picasso!" came the voice of a policeman, bellowing through a bullhorn. "Get down here!"

But Mickey wasn't about to be caught. Not tonight. He rappelled from the steel face of the freeway overpass and swung in a wide arc to the right. He stopped at the edge of his great painting and sprayed the initials "M.M." in bright red. It was a tag that was getting to be known around the city, as great masterpieces of spray-paint art appeared overnight.

Nobody knew who M.M. really was. But everyone knew what it stood for: Midnight Michelangelo.

Two policemen climbed the girder of the overpass to get him. He rappelled once more, his mountain harness holding him tight as he swung over to the left, like a human pendulum. Then he unhooked himself and scurried down a fence to freedom. Wendy was waiting for him. The police were confounded, trying in vain to pursue the boy but unable to catch up to him.

"Are you nuts, Mickey?" said Wendy. "Were those initials worth getting arrested for?" But Mickey only smiled. His head was pounding. The fumes from the spray paint gave him his headaches, he was sure, but his art was worth any amount of pain.

They were many blocks away when dawn began to break,

and Mickey had to turn back and look at his creation. The sun told a truth about his talent that the stark streetlights could not.

His work was a high-tech futurescape, filled with swooping monorails, bottomless steel canyons, glass skyscrapers reaching beyond the heavens, and sleek, silvery robotic faces. It covered the metal span of the overpass, looking down at the dull, urban sprawl around it. "It's incredible, Mickey," said Wendy. "*You're* incredible."

"It's my best yet," Mickey proudly told Wendy. As the sun grew brighter, the streaks of silver paint turned to gold.

"Every color has a voice, every texture a soul. . . ."

The next morning at school Mickey sat at his desk half asleep and tried to listen to Miss Clarkson spout forth her philosophy of art. But few kids in class were listening to their ninth-grade art teacher, and the ones that were really had no clue anyway. Paintbrush in hand, Mickey dozed off. He was startled awake by Miss Clarkson's tapping him roughly on the shoulder. She pointed to his blank canvas. "Working in white today?" she asked.

"Uh . . . I'm waiting for inspiration," answered Mickey.

Miss Clarkson smirked. "Inspiration requires consciousness, Mr. Blake."

Snickers erupted around the room, then a voice behind him whispered, "Guess you can't paint unless someone's filling out an arrest warrant, huh, Mickey?" It was Brody Harkin, of course. To Mickey, Brody was everything bad about the world. He was tall, handsome, arrogant, and brainless. He was also Wendy's boyfriend. Sure, Wendy might love Mickey's artwork, but it was Brody who had her attentions in every other way. Somewhere along the line, Wendy let it slip to Brody that Mickey was the Midnight Michelangelo. Ever since then, Brody taunted Mickey with the information—always threatening to announce it to the world. It was just one more frustration in a life that was anything but a picnic—but Mickey had learned to live with it. After all, lots of artists lived tortured lives, and Brody Harkin certainly qualified as torture.

Mickey tried to slip out quietly when the bell rang, but Miss Clarkson caught him and insisted he stay after class. He heard Brody snicker as he left the room, with his beefy arm slung over Wendy's shoulder.

"Someone oughta spray-paint *loser* on his forehead," Brody said.

Wendy threw Mickey an apologetic look, as if it was her job to apologize for Brody, and then she got lost in the crowd of students filing out of the room. Mickey continually wondered how Wendy could like a kid like Brody—but then Mickey figured it was that same poor judgment that made her hang around with *him* as well.

When everyone was gone, Mickey turned to Miss Clarkson. "I can explain about sleeping in class," he said. He was prepared to make up any and every excuse, except the truth, but Miss Clarkson would have none of it.

"I'm sure you can explain," she said. "You have a great imagination. Have you ever thought of putting it to good use?"

Mickey shrugged. "I have been."

"Yes," Miss Clarkson said with a frown, "but you can't make a living breaking the law . . . Michelangelo."

Hearing her say that name sent a high-tension chill weaving through his spine. Wendy knew about who he was, and so did Brody. There were other kids in school who suspected, but for a teacher to know—that meant trouble. The dull ache in his head began to pound with the fury of a jackhammer.

"Listen, Miss Clarkson, I've got a headache. I really have to go." He tried to slip out of the room, but Miss Clarkson stood in his way.

"Your work is great, Mickey," she told him. "I can spot it anywhere. I especially like the robot ninjas on the side of the unemployment office." Mickey thought she would make a move to get the principal, but she didn't. Could it be that she genuinely liked his work?

"You mean you won't tell?"

"I'm not the art police," she answered. "But I hate to see talent like yours going to waste."

That hurt. "Thousands of people see my stuff," Mickey said proudly.

"But they condemn it as trash," insisted Miss Clarkson. "*That's* the difference, Mickey—no one ever sandblasted the Sistine Chapel's ceiling."

Mickey looked down at his paint-stained shoes. "So?"

"So your work should be shown in galleries, winning awards. You should earn respect, not handcuffs."

Mickey scoffed and looked away, pretending he was bored, pretending he didn't care. But in truth, he was savoring every word she said. He closed his eyes and let the compliments sink in, hoping that maybe they'd drive his headache away.

"Your work has a soul, Mickey," she said. "It has a life of its own."

And neither of them knew how very true that was.

That afternoon, Mickey met Wendy at the Martians. It had gotten to be a habit, meeting in secret, because neither of them wanted Brody to know. "The Martians" was one of Mickey's best works. Red faces and bright, luminous eyes stretched the entire length of the wall. But today these martians would die.

"I tried to stop them, Mickey, but they wouldn't listen. They won't even admit it's art!" Wendy said to him as he arrived. "I'm sorry, Mickey. There was nothing I could do. They had already started when I got here. . . ."

"Started what?" Mickey rounded the corner to see workmen with paint rollers covering Mickey's martian masterpiece with dull gray paint; the same color as the rest of the city. His heart sank. What had taken him days in preparation and planning to create was thoughtlessly being destroyed in a matter of minutes. He winced at the sight. It felt as if they were painting the walls of his stomach. He could feel the pain in his head swell with his anger . . .

. . . and that's when he heard them. It was hollow and distant, but he heard them just the same.

The martians.

He could hear their muffled, wailing cries as they died, suffocated by the thick, greasy paint. But there was something more—for as he took another look at the martian faces, he could swear he saw them scowling darkly. He hadn't painted them like that. Their expressions had been glorious, not sinister.

"I . . . I didn't paint this," Mickey said.

"What? What do you mean?" said Wendy.

"These faces, they're all wrong." He moved closer to one of the twisted faces of the martians, and in the shadows of the painting he saw a hulking shape. It was dark, painted in deep burnt umber. The shadow had strange, serpentine coils and eyes like smoldering embers.

"What *is* that?" mumbled Mickey. But before he could have a better look, a workman painted it out of existence.

Mickey's mom wasn't an artist. Nor was she an art collector. Unless of course, you counted all the Elvis paintings she had bought from the Home Shopping Network. She was a single mom working two jobs, which didn't leave her much time for things like art. As for Mickey's dad, he had a new family in the suburbs and only came to visit Mickey around Christmastime—more to make himself feel better than out of any love for his skinny, brooding son. "Tis the season to feel guilty," Mickey had sung to his father when he picked him up last Christmas Day. Dear old Dad had not been amused by the truth.

But Mickey had his art—and *that* was something he could always count on. And so while Mom dozed in front of the TV each night, Mickey sat in his room, lovingly sketching the early drafts of the next great paintings he planned. Tonight's sketch was another alien landscape, this one full of tall, graceful creatures with silky, gossamer wings. They swooped and soared around crystalline towers. But tonight, Mickey couldn't keep his focus. Maybe it was the voices of the martians and the strangeness of their faces. It had to be his imagination, he decided—sleep deprivation can do weird things to the mind. Still, he couldn't stop thinking about it.

Even in the privacy of his room, there was something that didn't quite feel right. He kept imagining that some hideous, tentacled beast was just behind him, ready to grab him. But when he turned, there was nothing there but his rappelling harness hanging on his closet door. He tried to ignore the feeling, but he knew it was there, just like he knew he had seen a creature in his painting of the martians.

Four A.M. The brick wall of the building turned blood red and pale blue, then blood red again.

"Mickey, it's the police!" shouted Wendy.

The flashing light from the squad car painted the entire night red and blue. Mickey quickly hooked his spray cans onto his harness, ready to make a quick exit—but something was different tonight. His hand was shaking, but not from fear. It was trembling in a way he couldn't control. Wendy, standing on the fire escape beside him, reached out to him. "Come on, Mickey," she said desperately. He reached out to her, puzzled by his trembling hand. Why had his hand started shaking like that? And why now? He pulled the emergency release of his harness. But in his confusion, he pulled too soon. Mickey slipped out of Wendy's hand and fell three stories into a pile of trash bags, and into the arms of the Los Angeles Police Department.

He wouldn't call his mother—she didn't need this kind of trouble. Instead, he gambled and called the one person he felt he could trust. Luckily she showed up. Somehow, he knew he could count on the support of another artist. Miss Clarkson arrived at the police station less than half an hour after Mickey called.

"Are you the mother?" asked the cop on duty.

"His parents couldn't make it," said Miss Clarkson. "I'm his teacher."

The cop rolled his eyeballs.

"What is he supposed to have done?" demanded Miss Clarkson.

The cop crossed his arms. "You might say he painted the town red." Then he threw a nasty glance at Mickey. "Do you know how long we've been trying to catch this 'Midnight Michelangelo'?"

Miss Clarkson was too smart to ID Mickey to the police. "Are you kidding me?" she said.

"It's no joke," said the cop. "He's defaced half the city."

Miss Clarkson laughed. "Officer, you've seen those murals. Do you really think that a fourteen-year-old boy could do that?"

The cop, who a moment before seemed so sure of himself, began to stutter just a bit.

"Well, we caught him at the scene of the crime with a spray can."

Miss Clarkson shook her head and looked at the cop as if he was an idiot. "You caught him tagging, Officer. That's all."

Tagging? Mickey bristled at the suggestion. "I'm not a tagger," he said, insulted. But Miss Clarkson threw him a warning glance, and he shut up.

She turned back to the officer. "I think you've sufficiently traumatized this boy for a first offense. You can rest assured that his initials will go nowhere but on his homework from now on." Still the cop seemed unconvinced, until Miss Clarkson laughed again. "The Midnight Michelangelo! Are the police so desperate to find this guy that they have to pin it on a little kid?"

That did it.

"All right," conceded the officer. "Considering the kid's age, we're willing to cut him some slack. But I don't want to see him here again." Miss Clarkson grabbed Mickey and escorted him out.

They talked a lot on the drive home: about his talent, his troubles, his potential. But there was one thing Miss Clarkson asked that seemed to ring in his aching mind even after she had dropped him off at home. She had asked him how often he painted.

"Whenever the inspiration hits me," Mickey had told her.

Miss Clarkson had frowned. "I think your inspiration is your own worst enemy."

The next morning, Mickey noticed the vein.

He had woken up to another horrible headache—the way he had almost every day for the past month. He doused his face with cold water. Then, dragging a brush through his matted hair, he saw it. On his temple. A single vein. And as he looked at it, it seemed to spread, as if it was growing, pulsing, thick and purple. He gasped and slammed his eyes shut. Then, when he dared to open his eyes and confront his reflection, it was gone.

It's my stressed-out imagination, he told himself, *like the creature in the martians.* Playing it safe, he brushed his hair over his forehead where the spot had been. *It'll be all right,* Mickey told himself.

And everything *was* all right, until he approached the front steps of school. That's when he was confronted by a smiling Brody Harkin and his entourage of varsity lettermen and other assorted goons. "Mickey, I'm glad to see you're here," Brody said in a falsely concerned voice.

"Why wouldn't I be here?" muttered Mickey.

"After last night, I thought you might be in reform school or something," said Brody, loud enough to get the attention of just about every kid who was within shouting distance. They all turned to stare at Mickey.

"I don't know what you're talking about," mumbled Mickey. He tried to edge around Brody, but Brody's goons kept him from going anywhere.

"Sure you know what I'm talking about," said Brody. "Wendy told me all about it. I'm just glad you didn't get *her* arrested as an accomplice." There was a circle around them now. The same circle of kids that always seems to arrive before a fight.

"Excuse me, I've got class."

"Obviously not much," snorted Brody. The few kids around them who got the joke laughed out loud. Mickey could feel his head beginning to throb. He could feel that thick vein pulsing and wondered if everyone could see it.

"You don't want to mess with me today, Brody," Mickey warned.

Brody chuckled. "All right, tough guy," he said.

Mickey's headache continued to pound. "Listen, just get out

of my face. Why don't you go and smash some more cans on your forehead, or whatever you do for intellectual stimulation."

"You know why Wendy hangs out with you, don't you?" Brody said with a nasty hiss in his voice. "*Wendy feels sorry for you,* just like the rest of us."

Meltdown. Mickey lost it. He pounced on Brody, like a rabid, snarling dog. Brody clearly wasn't expecting it and was knocked down by the force of Mickey's pounce. They both crashed to the pavement. Mickey wasn't much for fighting, but few people had ever gotten him this angry. He windmilled his fists as hard and fast as he could, smashing them into Brody over and over again. And then, from the corner of his eye, he saw it. A tentacle suddenly appeared and coiled around Brody's neck. It squeezed tighter. Brody's face turned red. He was gasping. Far away, as if through a thousand layers of cotton, Mickey heard a voice.

"Mickey, stop it!" It was Wendy. He turned to look at her. She was standing next to him, screaming down at him, but he could barely hear her voice. "I said, stop it!"

When Mickey turned back to Brody, it wasn't a tentacle but his own hand that was squeezing Brody's throat. Shocked, Mickey pushed himself off Brody.

"Are you crazy?" screamed Wendy. "Are you out of your mind?"

Brody staggered to his feet, clutching his throat and gasping for air.

"Your charity case just turned into a basket case," he said in a hacking, wheezing tone.

Wendy went over to Brody to make sure he was okay. She put her arms around him, then kissed him. Mickey couldn't stand the sight of the two of them together.

Brody was right—Wendy just hung out with Mickey because she felt sorry for him, and now even *she* couldn't be trusted. After all, she must have been the one who had told Brody everything about last night.

"You two deserve each other!" Mickey shouted. Then he ran off. He was cutting school, but he didn't care. What did it matter now?

"Mickey, wait!" Wendy called to him, running. Finally she caught up with him, and he turned on her.

"Why don't you just write it all over the walls, Wendy? 'Mickey Blake just got arrested.' Here, I'll lend you a spray can."

"It wasn't like that," insisted Wendy. "Brody's dad's a lawyer. I told Brody because I thought he might help."

"What makes you think I need help?" shouted Mickey.

"Well, just look at you. It's not just what happened last night. You—you don't look right, Mickey. You've been acting weird." She grabbed him by the shoulder, forcing him to look her in the eye. "Something's wrong, isn't it?"

Almost as an afterthought he reached to touch the vein on his forehead, but it was gone.

"Mickey," she said. "Tell me what's wrong."

There was genuine concern in her voice. But the fact was, he didn't know what the problem was, or how deep it went.

Then Mickey's world grew one shade darker.

There was a commotion ahead of them. Crowds of people were huddled in front of a record store. They were all looking up at an outside wall—the same wall Mickey had started working on the night before . . . before he was taken away by the cops.

"That is, like, *so* cool," someone said.

Mickey looked up and had to grab a lamppost to keep himself from falling. *It was impossible.* There, before his eyes, was an immense horrorscape that covered the entire six-story brick wall. What was supposed to be beautiful birds had morphed into cruelly misshapen predators with steel fangs and flesh-shredding claws. Instead of a metropolis of delicate crystal spires, the raptors flew over a blighted ruin of a city. And there, even larger than before, a tentacled creature lurked in the shadows of the painting.

A policeman spoke with the shop owner.

"Don't worry," said the policeman. "We'll catch him sooner or later."

The shop owner laughed. "Catch him? I want to hire him. You can't buy this kind of promotion. This will sell a million CDs."

"Who do you think this guy is?" someone asked.

"I don't know," the shop owner shouted to the crowd, "but anyone who brings me this Midnight Michelangelo gets a free CD."

Mickey stood there feeling his eyes begin to glaze over. Wendy nudged him.

"Why don't you tell him? Maybe he'll pay you to do another one."

"But that's not what I painted," shouted Mickey. Then, Wendy turned to the crowd. "Hey! He's here. It's the Midnight Michelangelo!" Suddenly, Mickey was the center of attention, and the owner of the record store stormed through the crowd.

"You? You're gonna tell me this kid did *that* painting?"

Mickey shook his head. "No, no, it's a mistake. I didn't do it!"

"He goes out every night," explained Wendy. "He did the martians at the bus depot and the robots by the river—I was with him when he did it. Are you going to hire him like you said?"

Mickey turned to Wendy. "You were with me," he said. "You saw what I was painting, and it wasn't *that*!"

Wendy looked at the mural and shrugged. "I was up close. I couldn't see the whole thing."

Mickey began to panic. There *had* to be a way to prove what his painting was supposed to be. Then he realized he *did* have proof. He had his original sketch! He reached into his backpack, pulled it out, and unfolded it, showing it for everyone to see. "See! This is what I was painting last night, you see?" The crowd pressed forward to look at it and murmured in admiration. Some people applauded.

"I'll hire you for another one," said the record shop owner. "We'll work out the details later." Wendy looked at the crumpled piece of paper stretched between Mickey's shaking hands and gave him a half-grimace, half-smile.

"It certainly is . . . impressive," she said, "in a twisted sort of way."

Confused, Mickey turned to look at the paper himself. His hands, as badly as they were shaking, began trembling even more violently.

Because his sketch reflected the same bleak and awful mural in front of him.

"That is *so* cool, man," said someone behind him. Even the cop was getting into it.

"You know, some of us don't really want to catch you," the cop whispered into Mickey's ear. "To be honest, I kind of like those werewolves on the federal building."

"Werewolves?" said Mickey. "What werewolves?"

* * *

He walked home alone, but by the time he reached his block, he realized he was running. When he got to his room, he took every last sketch off his wall and out of every drawer and threw them away. Then he took every spray can he could find and tossed them into the trash. He wasn't satisfied until the trash was dumped down the garbage shoot, bound for his apartment building's incinerator.

All the while, he could hear the sounds in his aching head. A mocking laughter, the screech of far-off predators, and the wet, slithery sound of a tentacled creature moving closer.

The next morning, there was a mural on the lockers at school. Not just one locker, but spread across the entire hallway. It would have been bad enough if the mysterious mural was just your typical nightmare. But this one had a very special guest star: Brody Harkin.

In this mural, Brody was being mauled by a horrible clawed monster—half lobster, half human—but that wasn't the worst part, because in the mural's background a multi-tentacled beast looked on, eating popcorn. The creature, painted more clearly than before, looked like a cross between an octopus . . . and a human brain.

Wendy glared at the mural, and then at Mickey with an anger and disgust she had never shown him before. "Mickey, what is *wrong* with you? This is sick!"

"I had nothing to do with it!" screamed Mickey. "It wasn't me." But there in the corner were the initials, just like there always were. M.M. Midnight Michelangelo.

Brody stood before the perfect likeness of himself, and, amazingly, held his temper. Brody's friends quickly gathered in front of the mural, yelling, "Hey man, kick his butt!" And more kids arrived on the scene, joining in on the group rage, just wanting to see a fight. But Brody shook his head.

"What a wonderful 'work of art,' " Brody said with a bitter smile. "I want the principal to see this. I want the cops to see it." Then his million-dollar smile widened. "Thanks, Mickey," he said. "I couldn't have done a better job of getting you expelled."

Ignoring Brody, Mickey turned to Wendy, pleading. "I swear I didn't do it. I threw all my paint away yesterday. See! There's none left." He zipped open his backpack to prove it— but as he turned his pack upside-down, paint cans clattered out. Seven of them. Every color of the rainbow. Wendy turned and stormed away, leaving Mickey alone with his paint and his awful, awful mural.

Wendy didn't stick up for him. Miss Clarkson didn't stick up for him. Mickey was on his own this time, as he faced the principal.

"Young man, you have really asked for it. You trespassed after school hours, defaced school property . . . And look at the disruption you've caused your schoolmates. We have zero tolerance at this school—it's one strike and you're out. Do you know what that means, Mr. Blake?"

Mickey knew what it meant. "It means I'm expelled." Mickey held his throbbing head. It felt as if it would blow apart any second.

"You and your mother will meet with the school board, and we'll go from there. . . ."

Suddenly Mickey closed his eyes against the searing pain in his brain. He could feel the vein throbbing in his head. It felt as if something in his skull was trying to bang itself out. When Mickey opened his eyes, there was a tentacle rising over the chair behind the principal. He wanted to warn the man, but Mickey was frozen. He began to breathe in deep, sharp gasps.

"Are you all right, son? What's wrong?"

Tentacles loomed behind Principal Crenshaw, and one of them reached over, grabbed a pencil, and drew a ghoulish caricature of the principal on his own desk blotter. The tentacle signed it, "M.M.," and the beast let loose a deep, wet, slithery laugh.

But the principal heard nothing—saw nothing. Even when he turned and looked straight at the awful gray tentacle, he didn't see it.

Mickey got his breathing under control as the tentacle slithered away and disappeared. He knew what he had to do now—everything had suddenly become very clear. The principal turned away to call his mother, and the second he turned, Mickey slipped out the door and into the hallway.

A line of silver spray paint trailed down the empty school hall, and Mickey followed it. He tracked it to a doorway and down a creaky set of stairs, into the dank basement of the ancient school. It was a place littered with broken-down desks, battered shelves, and mildewed textbooks. Down here, every surface, every wall, every square inch, was covered with graffiti. Mickey heard the laughter again—the laughter of the beast.

"Where are you?" Mickey screamed. "Come out so I can see you." Something touched his face. He whirled to catch it, but there was nothing there. Nothing but a wet trail of slime on his cheek.

Mickey found a fire ax. It was mounted on brackets behind a glass barrier labeled EMERGENCY USE ONLY. Well, he thought, this certainly was an emergency. Mickey kicked the glass until it shattered, reached in, and took the ax in both hands.

"Hey, slimeball!" he shouted, "I've got something for you!"

In the dark recess he could hear the tantalizing hiss of a spray can. He inched forward, looking from side to side, searching for the beast that had grown in the shadow-painted corners of his own head.

"Come out, come out, wherever you are!" he shouted. Mickey laughed at his own ridiculousness. The furnace came on and shuddered violently, then let out a deep rumble.

Something moved! Mickey turned and swung, knocking over a pyramid of paint cans. They spilled a rainbow of colors across the floor. Again, he heard the laughter.

"Missed me, missed me! Now you gotta kiss me!" it chanted in its throaty, gurgling voice. It only made Mickey angrier. Too angry to hold back his fury. He swung the ax in every direction, splintering a desk, cleaving a filing cabinet in two, smashing an old chalkboard until finally he found the monster standing against the round tank of the rusty boiler.

It was awful. A gray mass of throbbing brain tissue, and from it grew thick tentacles—nerve endings that thrashed and flailed like snakes. But worst of all were its eyes. Two pinpoints of red light in a cloud of gray matter.

"Don't do it, Mickey," the creature taunted. Mickey raised his ax. *"You'll be sorry!"* said the creature. But Mickey couldn't stop himself. He swung the blade in a high arc and brought the ax down with all his might.

He heard a scream. A girl's scream. The blade embedded in the boiler with a hollow clang and a blast of white steam— right next to the face of . . .

. . . Brody Harkin!

The creature had tricked him, and the blade of the axe had missed Brody by less than an inch. Behind him Wendy screamed again, as Brody scrambled away in terror.

"Stop him!" screamed Wendy. "Somebody stop him!"

What little sanity Mickey held onto was gone. The mocking

laughter in his head was now unbearable. He pulled the blade from the boiler.

"You missed me!" the creature screamed in his head. *"Accept it, Mickey, you'll never kill me!"* He saw it there again, in the shadows, and he raised his ax to strike it . . . but then he had a better idea. He threw his ax down, opened his backpack, and pulled out a spray can for each hand.

"Oh, you're going to paint me?" taunted the creature. *"Be sure to get my good side."* The creature turned to show its profile and smiled that slimy brain smile.

"Hold that pose," said Mickey. Then he let loose from both spray cans, dousing the creature in a blue-black fog. It laughed again, unbothered by the paint dripping down into the crevices of its cortex—not caring about the jumble of smashed paint cans and spilt enamel that it stood in. But Mickey continued spraying. He sprayed a line of paint from the monster to the hot furnace, like a fuse, and as soon as the wet paint touched the furnace, it caught fire.

The creature realized the danger too late. *"No!!!"*

The flame raced down the paint-fuse toward the puddle of flammable enamel, and instantly the creature burst into flames. It let out an awful, dying wail as it burned, and finally it dissolved into the swirls of burning paint. That was the last thing Mickey remembered before he lost consciousness.

He woke up in a hospital room with his mother beside him holding his hand and Wendy on his other side. His head hurt something awful. "Is it gone?" Mickey asked weakly.

"You're going to be all right," Wendy said. "They got the tumor in time." Mickey had to think very slowly and clearly about what she was saying. Only now did he realize that his head was tightly bandaged.

"Tumor?"

"Yes," said a doctor looking down at him, smiling as doctors do. "One nasty brain tumor," he said. "The good news is that we got the whole thing, and we took it out without damaging any of the surrounding tissue. You're a very lucky young man."

Mickey's mom burst into tears.

"You're going to be all right, Mickey," she said. "You're going to be all right."

"In a way," said Wendy, "you tried to tell us. . . . Going out and painting those 'things,' then not remembering you did it. The doctor said it was your subconscious trying to warn us."

Mickey took a deep breath. He supposed he could wrestle with himself forever, trying to figure out whether the creature was real or just a hallucination brought on by a tumor. But thinking about that was a sure way to madness. The important thing was that the monster was out of his head, and out of his life for good. It was a memory he was happy to paint over, and lose forever.

Wendy gently held his hand. "I'm sorry about those nasty things I said to you."

Mickey smiled. "Hold that pose," he said, never wanting this moment with Wendy to end.

Meanwhile, deep down in the hospital basement, a med student tended to the pathology lab. With a sandwich in one hand and a medical instrument in the other, he studied a small, fleshy mass that had settled at the bottom of a jar of formaldehyde. It was a lump of brain tissue, with spidery, tentacle-like dendrites. The label on the jar read: M. BLAKE.

"So that's a brain tumor," the med student mumbled to himself. "That is one ugly sucker."

He put down his sandwich to clean up the table and then picked it up again on his way out. He didn't notice that the jar of formaldehyde was now empty. He didn't notice that there was something moving between the slices of his bread as he took a bite of his sandwich.

But a few minutes later, he did notice a sudden headache coming on.

RALPHY SHERMAN'S INSIDE STORY

•••

Of course you don't have to believe it, but this is a true story. As true as my dad being a spy, and my mom being abducted by aliens. And if you don't believe me, you can ask my sister.

I suppose I should start before the frogs and the ants. I suppose I should start even before my cousins arrived.

As usual, Dad was away on top-secret business when we got news that my cousins were coming, and Mom, well, we haven't seen her much since she was taken from our time-space continuum. So it was only me, my sister Roxanne, and our new nanny all alone in our immense house. (Actually, our nannies are always new, because none of them has ever lasted more than a couple of weeks, can't say why.) At any rate, we got E-mail from Aunt Millicent and Uncle Bernard that they were going on vacation, and since we had our big, empty house all to ourselves, could we watch our darling little cousins for them?

"Gag me," said Roxanne when she read the note. "I think I'm gonna hurl breakfast."

I knew how she felt, but Olga the nanny had no sense of the problem.

"Dey are your cousins," she said in a thick accent. She was from a country whose name I couldn't pronounce even if you paid me in rubles. "You should be happy to see your cousins."

To which I replied, "You don't know Candida and Bratt."

"Nonsense—I cannot wait to meet them," Olga chimed. "They cannot be worse than the two of you." Which in most cases, would probably be true—after all, most of our nannies leave with a scream, rather than a smile on their lips, can't say why. But rumor has it that Bratt and Candida had populated entire mental institutions with the mentally—and sometimes physically—shattered remnants of their former nannies.

Roxanne and I counted the days until they arrived, like convicts numbering the days till execution. Two weeks . . . one week . . . and finally the dreaded day was here. Similar to the beginning of most natural disasters, I could hear the neighborhood dogs bark as their car pulled up in front of our house. The doorbell rang, and we found them there, deposited on our doorstep, with three trunks. It looked as if they were prepared for a long siege.

Aunt Millicent was already running back to the car, which Uncle Bernard kept impatiently idling by the curb. "I'm sure you'll all have a wonderful time together," lied Aunt Millicent, trying to brush Bratt's sticky fingerprints off her mink as she ran. She leapt into the car, and Uncle Bernard burned rubber even before the door was closed, in no small hurry to escape.

So here they were, standing in our foyer. Seven-year-old

Candida was in her typical pink frilly dress, looking like a grinning fugitive from "It's a Small World." She had a smile from ear to ear and looked like a human happyface. Beside her stood five-year-old Bratt. His hair was even messier and his face dirtier than I remembered, which was quite an accomplishment. His real name had once been Brett, but so many people called him Bratt that even his parents started calling him that. In fact, they might have had his name legally changed, although I'm not certain. In any case, there stood Bratt with his left index finger lodged so deeply into his nose that he was pulling boogers from the next county.

"Well, hello!" chimed Olga the nanny, throwing out her foreign arms to greet my cousins as if they were normal children. Bratt gave her a grimace, revealing his missing front teeth.

"I'm bored," he said. "This place is boring. And you're ugly."

Although Olga made no move to deny the charge, she was not thrilled by the observation.

Candida shook her head with a broad, knowing smile.

"Bratt," she said, "you're so *incorrigible.*" Which is one of the tamer words people used to describe Bratt. Then Candida turned to my sister. She ratcheted her smile up a few notches. "Hey, Roxanne," she said brightly. "I brought my 'Golly Miss Molly HappyTime Plastic Tea Set.' Let's go have a tea party!"

Roxanne narrowed her eyes to slits. "I'd rather die," she said, but Candida just giggled happily.

"Oh, Roxanne, you're so funny!" she said. "Isn't she funny, Helga?"

"Olga," corrected our nanny.

"Whatever!" said Candida, and she dragged Roxanne into the den for Chinese tea torture. As for Bratt, he was already swinging from the chandelier.

*   *   *

The day quickly became a festival of shattered glass and splintered wood, compliments of Bratt. Five broken banister rails, four demolished vases, three shredded sofas, two dented appliances, and that weird-looking bird he nailed with a baseball in our pear tree. At first, poor Olga tried to clean up after him, but not even her days as an Olympic wrestler could prepare her for this challenge. As for Candida, she was accustomed to making her way through Bratt's mounting debris, and she flitted around the house with a carefree smile so bright, you needed sunscreen. This was all to be expected—you have to understand, this was normal for our cousins. It was at dinner that things started to get weird.

Olga, rather than put up with Bratt's nagging, agreed to serve us all his favorite thing for dinner. Lamb-aroni. It was while we were picking through our Lamb-aroni that a frog fell out of nowhere into Bratt's bowl. Tomato sauce splattered onto everyone.

"What is this?" said Olga. "Who has dropped a frog into the Lamb-aroni?"

"Oops!" said Bratt. Then he grabbed the frog, tomato sauce and all, and put it in his shirt pocket. This wouldn't have bugged me in the least, because after all, Bratt has been known to bring worse things than frogs to the table with him. But you see, Bratt didn't have a frog in his pocket when he sat down, and for the life of me I had no idea where that frog had come from.

Then that night, while we were watching sing-along videos (at Candida's request of course), another strange thing made an appearance in the room. I saw it out of the corner of my eye as it came hurtling across the room, bouncing with a *clink* off the glass of the TV. Olga picked it up and examined it. It was a tiny glass unicorn, perfectly molded, and just the size of your fingernail

"How beautiful," she cooed. "Isn't that nice." But when she asked us whose it was, nobody claimed it.

It was as we were getting ready for bed that Roxanne pulled me aside and whispered to me.

"I don't know where that thing came from," she said, "but I do know one thing: Candida sneezed just before it hit the TV."

Around three in the morning, I was awakened by something cold and slimy hopping across my face. I brushed it away and sat up in bed. For a moment I thought it was a dream. But then I saw the covers undulating. I flung back the covers to find . . .

. . . frogs!

Not just one frog or two, but a dozen of them, hopping madly in every direction. It was almost biblical, if you know what I mean. A plague of frogs. I bailed out of bed.

"Oh, Olga!" I called. "Amphibian alert!"

Olga came running. When she saw the plague, she raced around trying to catch the frogs with a trash basket, but her efforts were wasted. There were simply too many of them . . .

. . . and that's when I noticed where they were coming from. I was sharing my room with Bratt tonight. I had the lower bunk, he had the upper, and the frogs were all hopping down from his bed. The little snot-bucket had taken an entire collection of frogs to bed with him and didn't tell anyone!

Roxanne stood in the doorway, not wanting to join in our frogathon. And through all this, little Bratt slept, his mouth open and drooling.

Candida arrived dragging her Raggedy Ann doll by its red-yarn head. "Oh, I'll take care of it," she said. We were all more than happy to let her deal with her brother's plague of frogs. "My poor brother," she said, "he really is a holy terror sometimes."

"There's nothing 'holy' about it," mumbled Roxanne.

Olga made Roxy and me some hot chocolate, and we left Candida alone to contend with the frogs. She got rid of them somehow, but I had no idea where she put them.

In the morning it was Roxanne's turn.

"Oh, yuck! No way!" Her yells woke me up at dawn, and I hurried into her room. There was a colony of ants running in black rivers up and down her walls and covers. But if Roxanne was tormented by ants, it was nothing compared to what they were doing to Candida, who had just awakened in the spare bed. You could barely see her beneath the moving army of insects.

"Oh! Oh! Dear me!" cried Candida, while Roxanne screeched out much more colorful words.

It took three cans of Raid and half the day to rid the house of the ants.

"Where did they come from?" Olga kept mumbling as she sponged ant guts off the wall, but I knew *that* wasn't the question we ought to be asking. The question was *why* had they come. This whole situation was a nuisance, and it was irritating to have nuisances that we didn't create. Roxanne took it upon herself to solve the mystery, while I spent the day chasing after Bratt.

I used to think that I had mastered being a pain in the rear, but I really have to hand it to Bratt: He is the true baron of butt pain.

"See, I can play golf," he said as he ran off swinging the club like a midget samurai. He proceeded to decapitate every plant in our garden.

"See, I can drive!" he said as he backed Dad's precious sports car out of the garage . . . and right into the fountain.

"See, I can swim good," he said and dove head first into a scummy, stagnant pond in the woods behind our property. I think it was the pond that finally slowed him down, because just before dinner, he claimed to feel sick.

"Feel my throat," he ordered me. "Do I got swollen glands?" He showed his neck to reveal so many dirt rings that you could probably tell his age by counting them, like a tree. I reached out to feel his glands.

They were swollen all right, but there was something else about them that wasn't right, because as I held them beneath my thumb and forefinger . . . *I could swear they were moving*.

There was something strangely familiar about the feel of Bratt's swollen glands. They reminded me of something that I couldn't quite place. . . .

Shortly before dinner, Roxanne came out of hiding to report her findings to me. You see, she had been avoiding Candida all day because Candida wanted Roxanne to play with her Dental Hygienist Barbie. Roxanne would rather have swallowed hot coals.

Roxanne called me into the den and shoved a little glass vial under my nose.

"Sniff this," she said, "and tell me what it smells like."

I took a deep whiff and cringed. It was an aroma all too familiar. "Candida!" I said. "It smells like Candida. What is it?"

Roxanne leaned closer to me and whispered, "Equal amounts of cinnamon, ginger, and nutmeg. Plus a pinch of ground clove."

I wrinkled my forehead, not getting it. "That's weird."

"But that's not all. Take a look at this!" She revealed a small cup and inside were tiny, white, crystalline granules.

"What is it?" I asked.

"Taste it."

Reluctantly, I dipped my finger into the cup and lifted it to my mouth. The taste was unmistakable.

"Sugar!"

"It was all over Candida's sheets," Roxanne told me. "That's why the ants came."

"Candida went to bed with candy?" I suggested.

Roxanne shook her head. "Are you kidding me? Little Miss Perfect doesn't even eat candy."

I thought it all through. There had to be a good explanation for this. "Sugar and spice . . ." I mumbled.

". . . and everything nice," added Roxanne. She opened her palm to reveal a whole menagerie of tiny glass figurines—the kind that seemed to fly across the room every time Candida sneezed. "That's what little girls are made of."

My jaw dropped as it all began to come together, and I realized what Roxanne was trying to tell me. It made sense in its own strange and unusual way. I tried to recall what the matching nursery rhyme for boys was, and although I couldn't recall the whole thing, I remembered enough of it, and now it finally dawned on me exactly what Bratt's moving, swollen glands felt like.

They felt like snails.

Suddenly a cry rang out from the backyard, and Candida ran inside in a panic. For the first time in her life the smile had left her face. I hardly recognized her.

"You have to help! Hurry! Bratt's hurt himself really bad. Inga!" she called "Inga!"

"Olga," I corrected, and calmed her down long enough to find out what had happened. Apparently her little brother was out back chasing squirrels with a pitchfork when he tripped and had the kind of accident that only happens in a mother's nightmares.

We all ran out back to help our poor little cousin. Bratt was lying in the grass, crying his eyes out. He had a big hole in his side where the pitchfork had speared him, but he wasn't bleeding. Not a drop. Instead, he was wallowing in a pool of frogs and snails and furry, squirming things that I could not identify.

"What are those?" I asked, pointing.

Bratt snuffled, then shouted at me, "They're puppy dog tails, butthead!"

Well, Olga took one good look at those tails and she was a nanny no more. She turned and ran off into the sunset and we haven't seen her since.

Meanwhile, Bratt's condition had gotten serious. Bratt's three primary ingredients were hopping, slithering, and squirming away faster than any one of us could catch them.

"We have to get him to the hospital!" screamed Candida. "He'll need a transfusion."

And although I shuddered to think where they would get enough puppy dog tails for a transfusion, I did as I was told. I called 911 and put it in the hands of the paramedics.

Modern medicine is an amazing thing. I don't know how the doctors did it, but they had Bratt stitched up and shipped back to us in less than a week.

His parents, having heard about the accident, reluctantly cut their 'round-the-world vacation short.

A week after the accident, we all sat at the breakfast table together. Candida sat primly, eating Shredded Wheat like a good little girl, and Bratt scarfed down Sugar-Frosted Cookie Dough cereal. Everything was back to normal.

"Well," said Uncle Bernard ruffling Bratt's tangled hair, "sounds like you had quite an adventure!"

"It stunk," grumbled Bratt. "The hospital was even more boring than here." Bratt hiccuped, and a small tree frog hopped from his mouth into the cereal.

"Don't open your mouth so wide dear," said his mother. She

scooped up the frog and popped it back into her son's mouth. "It's rude."

Uncle Bernard sipped his coffee, then frowned. "A little sweeter," he said. Then he tipped Candida's head, and a stream of sugar ran from her left ear into his coffee. "I think you've learned your lesson, Bratt," he said. "No playing with pitchforks unless it's under adult supervision."

Bratt only grunted and continued to gum his soggy cereal.

It was as they were leaving that I asked the final question that would solve the last remaining riddle about my cousins' unique family.

"Candida?" I asked as they were heading out the door. "How is it that your parents can afford a 'round-the-world vacation?"

"That's simple," she said. "My parents are made of money."

Which explains why they jingle when they walk.

HE OPENS A
WINDOW

●●●

You must never pull back the curtains," the kindly old woman always says. "You must never look out the window." Anna knows why it must be so; to risk anyone seeing her and her two young sisters will mean death or something worse. And so for many months Anna has obeyed, not daring to let anything but the faintest hint of daylight into the room. The old woman brings them food. Hearty stews when meat can be found, and undersized vegetables when that is all to be had, but always the best from the old woman's table.

"When will we see Momma and Poppa?" Gretchen, her youngest sister, asks. She is only four, and not old enough to understand that the answer might be "never."

"Soon," Anna tells her, and she tries to make herself believe it. Segrid, who is seven, looks up to Anna wide-eyed with hope. Hope of seeing their parents is all that keeps them going in this small, locked room that has become their lives.

The boy's father is a soldier, and his mother long buried.

The grocer keeps a bed for him at the back of the store, in exchange for delivering groceries twelve hours a day, throughout the wartime streets of Hamburg. When regiments of soldiers march past the boy, he always thinks he sees his father among them. He is hopeful, but even more, he is frightened by the dark soldiers he knows bring nothing but death. He can't stand to think of his father as one of them.

Or himself. He is fourteen now. If the war continues, he will be absorbed into the ranks of soldiers, to fight and die for the fatherland.

There used to be many children in Hamburg, but there are fewer now. Some families took refuge in the countryside when the war began, and others were driven from their homes and taken away in overcrowded buses and trains. Jews, mostly.

They were brought to the countryside, too, then thrown into the dark, mysterious camps, never to be seen again. He has lost many friends that way. Boys he had played with in the street, girls whose hands he longed to hold. He will not cry for them, because he knows if he starts crying, he may never stop.

There are some of them, though, that remain like ghosts, haunting the secret places of other peoples' homes.

Like the old woman's house on Baumeister Street.

He knows there are children hiding there, because he delivers enough vegetables and fruits for a family, although only one old woman is supposed to live there. And before he knocks, he often hears the faint whisper of children's voices from an upstairs window. So he is always sure to throw in some extra food without letting the grocer know.

Today as he approaches the old woman's door, he has some

cabbages and onions slipped from under the grocer's nose while he wasn't looking ... but today he hears no children's voices upstairs, and notices something strange about the house. He has been here enough to know that there are three upstairs windows—the center one always hidden behind heavy, dark curtains that never open. But today there are no curtains. In fact, today, there is no third window—only the bricks of the house where the window should be.

In Anna's eight-by-eight-foot world, strange things are happening. The thin hint of light that sneaks into the room has begun to change day to day. Her sisters don't notice, but Anna does. She has lived in Hamburg all her life and knows every color of the sky, from the pale clouds of winter, to the blue hues of summer, to the flickering night glow of lamplight. But lately the light peeking beneath the closed curtains is all wrong. One day the light seems red as fire, the next day green and shimmering, as if seen through the ocean. One day it's purple, and the next, there's no light at all. She doesn't dare tell the old woman, for Anna's certain it's just the madness of life in this room that's making her see these things.

But the sounds have been changing, too.

Some days, when the light is normal, she will hear cars in the street, and the terrible marching of soldiers. But on other days will come the caws of birds she can't identify, and the bellows of far-off beasts that cannot reside in Hamburg.

Until now, she has not dared to pull back the curtains and peek outside—but today is different from those days before, because the old woman has brought them neither breakfast nor lunch, and Anna begins to worry. The old woman had left for an early morning walk, but these days no streets are safe. Anna never heard her come back, and she fears the worst. Their secret room is locked from the outside, and if the woman doesn't return, they will have no way to get out. The only exit is through the window, in full sight of anyone and everyone who might turn them over to the Nazis. . . .

Yet she wonders if there are any Nazis at all outside her window today; because at this moment, a bright purple light peeks from beneath the curtains. It should be long past dusk but the window hints at an unearthly light of day. Even Gretchen notices it.

"It's like the sky has forgotten how to be blue," she says.

Finally Anna dares to do something she hasn't done for the five months she has been in the room. She reaches out her fingers, slips them between the thick fabric of the old curtains, and parts them wide enough to get a single eye's view of the outside world.

What she sees makes her dizzy. It makes her grip onto the curtain to keep herself from falling.

"What is out there?" asks Gretchen. "Are there troops? Are they going to find us?"

"No," says Anna in a whisper.

Just outside the window, there are dense purple clouds billowing heavenward and downward, stretching to the horizon. There is no earth out there. There is no Hamburg—only the purple clouds of a world Anna could never dare imagine. It's as if their tiny room is floating alone in some strange corner of heaven.

The boy gets no grocery orders from the old woman on Baumeister Street that day, or the next—no requests for the usual tomatoes, onions, and apples. Although part of him feels that she must have found a market she likes better, he knows this woman well enough to know that her habits define her.

And what troubles him even more is the missing window.

He can think of a few logical reasons for the window to be

gone. Perhaps it had been closed in and the wall built to cover it—that could be done in a day. But as the window faces Baumeister Street, such remodeling would be certain to get the attention of the Gestapo. Or perhaps the window had never been there at all, in spite of his many memories of it. He would much rather believe his own mind has become faulty than believe the window has simply disappeared. True, disappearance has become a commonplace thing since the Nazis came to power, but this disappearance is different from any of the mysteries of the Third Reich.

And so he goes to the old woman's house, day after day, until the window finally reappears.

Three days with no food.

There is a sink and running water, but it hardly helps the hunger pangs. Her sisters complain continuously, and Anna does her best to quiet them, all the while thinking of the world beyond the window.

Gripping her stomach, Anna peers out through the curtains once more. It's different now. The mystical clouds have been replaced by an arid desert. Parched, cracked earth stretches toward a horizon, the sky the same vermilion red as the sand. It looks bleak and hot . . . still, it's more inviting than the room and the world behind the closed door.

She realizes she must have lost her mind to see such wondrous things, but if so, then she's not the only one, because her sisters have squeezed their way between the curtains and see the strange landscape as well.

"Who put that there?" says Gretchen, too young to know the impossible when she sees it. Segrid only looks to Anna, expecting some rational explanation, but Anna has none to give.

An hour later, the light beneath the curtains changes again, and Anna can't stop herself from looking. She has become addicted to the dazzling vistas that change like slides of places she will never visit. She pulls back the curtains, wider this time so that she might see with both eyes rather than just one whatever stunning view lies beyond the pane.

But to her dismay, there are only the gray cobblestones of the Hamburg street. Instantly she realizes her folly and how her own curiosity has led to her end . . .

. . . because down in the street, a boy looks up at her. His gaze holds her, and neither of them can look away. There is warmth in his eyes, and honesty. Even from a distance she feels she can trust him not to turn them in to the authorities, but in these strange days, she knows that no one is to be trusted.

She closes the curtain and prays that the boy's heart does not belong to the Nazis.

A tall man in a dark uniform waits in the grocery store for the boy.

The boy's heart seizes with unexpected joy, because he is certain it must be his father . . . but as the man turns, the boy sees nothing familiar in his face, except for the familiar stone-cold eyes of the Gestapo.

The man has been talking to the grocer—and now the grocer will not look the boy in the face. He only casts his eyes down as the Gestapo officer removes his leather gloves and saunters toward the boy. He smiles, but his smile is anything but warm.

"Herr Grottmann tells me you've been stealing food."

The boy thinks quickly. He can't afford a single error. "Herr Grottmann is mistaken," the boy says. "I only eat the food he gives me."

"I'm not talking about the food you eat," says the Gestapo officer, "I am talking about the food you give away." He grabs the boy by the arm firmly enough to leave bruises from his crushing fingertips. Then he pulls him into the back office.

"You could be a hero or you could be a traitor," the Gestapo officer announces. He has seated the boy in a chair in the small, windowless office—and although he speaks softly, there is poison in his voice.

"All you have to do is tell me who you've been stealing food for."

The boy wrinkles his nose. The man's breath smells like cigarettes and decay. It smells like death.

"I deliver what Herr Grottmann gives me. If food is missing, it's his doing, not mine."

But the hard man sees through his lie with his dangerous eyes. "We know there are many enemies of the state in hiding. We also know you are bringing them food." He takes a long drag on his slim cigarette and blows the acrid smoke into the air. "Believe me, if you don't turn them in, we will find them without you . . . and when we do, you'll be sent to the concentration camps with them."

He has heard stories about what unthinkable things go on in the camps, though he doesn't want to believe them. And all he has to do to be free of this man is tell about the girl he saw today, peeking out through the blinds of the window that wasn't always there. But he can't imagine how this girl could possibly deserve the punishment that would be dealt to her.

"I'm sorry, sir," says the boy, "but I know no enemies of the state."

The interrogation ends as quickly as it began.

"Very well," says the man dismissively. "We will search every home on your delivery list until we find them."

And as soon as the officer leaves, the grocer, wanting no more trouble, fires the boy and sends him packing.

The boy doesn't worry about himself now. He hurries to the home on Baumeister Street, hoping that the window will be there when he arrives. It was there that morning, and a girl was behind it—thirteen or fourteen by the looks of her. Afraid, he runs all the way there. He doesn't know that he is being followed.

A view of Earth.

A sight so wondrous, Anna and her sisters lose their breath in the awe of the moment as they look through their strange and magical window. Wind whistles around the window frame into the vacuum of space. The glass of the window can barely contain the air in the room.

They must be millions of miles into space, and the globe before them looms peaceful and serene. Hard to imagine that this serene world could hold the pain and turmoil of this terrible war.

Then comes the sound from downstairs. At first, it seems like loud knocking—but in a moment she realizes that someone is kicking the door down. Anna lets the curtains fall, hiding the view from space.

Finally they hear the doorjamb splinter, and her sisters begin to wail. If there had been any way to save themselves, it is gone now. Heavy footsteps pound up the stairs, and in a moment the door explodes with the force of a heavy black boot.

Four guards scream at them in loud frightening voices. "Get up—let's go—hurry up!"

And then another voice. A young one.

"I'm sorry," the voice says. "I didn't mean to . . . they followed me!"

Anna spins around to see the boy in the iron grip of another nameless soldier. "I'm sorry," he says again. And in spite of her fear, Anna knows he is telling the truth. He had not meant to bring this fate upon them.

A guard grabs Gretchen, wrenching her off the radiator coil. The curtain ruffles a bit as he pulls her away. . . .

And suddenly, Anna realizes what she must do.

Still in the grip of the guard, she reaches out and pulls the curtain wide to reveal the star-filled space beyond the window.

In an instant, the guards and the boy turn to gape at the harsh Earth-light passing through the window.

"What is this?" says one of the guards, amazed by the wondrous sight.

Anna can waste no time now. She grabs the closest thing to her heavy enough to do the job: a picture of her parents—the only one she has left—surrounded by a heavy silver frame.

She wrenches free from the guard, grabs her sisters in with one arm, and with the other hurls the silver-framed picture at the window.

The whistling of air around the closed window explodes into an angry gale as the glass shatters and the air from the room sucks into the vacuum of space.

The four guards, unprepared, are barely able to utter a scream before they are sucked out of the room and into space. They spin end over end into the void, their screams silenced by the cosmos, where there is no air, no sound, and no life. Anna knows she may die as well, but this death is better than death in the camps.

Anna's hand is clenched tightly on the hot, hot radiator coil while her other hand desperately grips onto her sisters. The racing wind lifts her off the ground as it pours in through the broken door and out the shattered window. She can feel the pipe of the radiator begin to strain with her weight.

"Here! Grab my hand!"

The voice screams out against the violent wind. It is the boy! His hand tightly grips the doorknob, though his feet are dangling in midair, pulled by the wind, just as Anna's are.

"The radiator won't hold you!" he yells. "Grab my hand!"

Anna swings her arm away from the radiator and into the

boy's hand, just as the radiator tears free from the floor and steam explodes from the wall. The radiator hits the window, smashing what's left of its frame, and disappears into orbit.

The boy grasps the doorknob. He knows his hands are strong, but not strong enough to survive in a force such as this. Finally the wind tears him from the knob and hurls him and the girls toward the window—and although he feels fear at the thought of his own death, greater still is the sorrow that these girls who have suffered so long in this room must also die.

He waits for the air to be sucked from his lungs . . . he waits for the cold of space . . . but instead he hits the floor with a heavy bump. And all is silence.

It is a long time before he can open his eyes, and when he does, the room is filled with a soft, green light.

The oldest girl stands, holding her crying sisters in her arms, and peers out the window. The boy stands beside her to see a rolling landscape of strange purple trees and green, glowing skies. They do not question each other, because they know no answer would ever be good enough.

Instead, the boy turns to the girl. "My name is Friedrich," he tells her.

"I'm Anna." She glances out the shattered window once more. "Will you come, or will you stay?" she asks him.

The decision is easier for him than he thought it would be. In a world of many dark unknowns, here is an unknown filled with hope.

They step out, and into the strange world of unfamiliar sights, smells, and sounds.

Gretchen and Segrid have stopped crying. Their eyes now follow the path of a blue butterfly the size of a kite across the sky.

She turns around to see the window disappear forever, sealing out the hopelessness of the small room. For five months the door to that room had been locked. Her parents once told her that when God closes a door, he opens a window. But they could never have dreamed of such a deliverance as this.

There will be peace here, Anna knows. Peace and freedom ... and time. She is glad Friedrich has chosen to come ... and yet there is a sadness without measure that fills her, and always will.

She cries as she thinks of the many small rooms and dark hiding places that know no such windows ... and she cries for her parents whose memory spins through space in a silver frame, lost but not forgotten, in the powerful current of eternity.

CLOTHES MAKE
THE MAN

●●●

An alarm blasts.

Then the carousel jerk-starts, slowly turning around and around. It's not the kind of carousel you find at the amusement park, but the kind you find in airports—that stainless-steel mechanical thingamabob that sends the luggage on a slow ride around and around the baggage claim area.

"What's taking so long?" barks my father impatiently as other people's suitcases come flying out of the dark chute. My father is an annoyed traveler. I don't know if he's like that when it comes to business travel, but whenever we come along, *everything* annoys him. There's a food cart in the aisle when he wants to go to the bathroom, for instance. Or the seat won't recline. Or our luggage is late in arriving.

"Logan, you and Leslie go to the other side of the carousel, and if our bag comes out that side, let me know."

My sister, Leslie, rolls her eyes at me as we trudge off to the other side. With my father, it's like a competition—an Olympic sport. We have to get our luggage and escape from the airport before all the other travelers, or we lose.

"Ah, he's just upset that our vacation's over," I tell Leslie. To be honest, so am I. Maui was like another world compared to Cleveland. And tomorrow we're supposed to go back to school with five-hour jet lag. What fun.

Dozens of people, wearing heavy winter coats over their flowery Hawaiian shirts, fight for space at the far end of the carousel. Since Leslie and I are smaller, we weave our way in between them and get to the front, where we have a clear view of the baggage slide. Mom and Dad's bag is the first of our luggage out—a big monster of a suitcase that barely fits through the hole. Leslie's is next—a little flowery thing Grandma got her last year.

I wait . . . and wait . . . and wait.

Across the carousel I can see Dad impatiently tapping his foot.

"Next time, we're packing everything in two big bags," he proclaims as he comes around to wait with me. "No more waiting around for little cases." He shakes his head disgustedly. I guess it's *my* fault the luggage handlers haven't gotten to my bag yet.

The crowd thins out as we wait. Outside, twilight quickly becomes night, and still my bag hasn't arrived.

"It figures," fumes Dad. He glances at his watch for the billionth time, and I grin. "Don't worry, Dad, it's only two in the afternoon . . . Hawaii time." Pretty funny. Until I notice that my dad isn't laughing.

He quickly adjusts his watch to Ohio time.

Finally, after every other bag has been pulled off the carousel and the rest of our flight has left the baggage claim area, my bag is spit out of the hole and slides down toward us.

"Hallelujah!" My dad throws up his hands and says, "Grab it, and let's go."

I pick up the bag. Although I crammed it full of souvenir seashells and a million other things, it feels light—but Dad is already storming his way out of the terminal with Mom and Leslie, so I don't have time to think about it. I just hurry along after him, pulling my suitcase behind me.

"You mean, you got the wrong suitcase?"

Leslie and I are still up that night around two in the morning. Mom and Dad are zonked out, and are snoring away, but Leslie and I aren't so lucky. Since I can't sleep, I figure I'd unpack—but when I zip open the case, nothing inside looks familiar.

Leslie reaches in, and pulls out a leather glove. "Aren't these your gloves?"

"No. Why would I take gloves to Maui?"

I pull out layer after layer of clothes. They're kids clothes all right, but not this kid's. I search for the address label attached to the handle, but there isn't one.

"You're gonna have to tell Dad," Leslie says.

The idea doesn't thrill me. Telling Dad will open up a nasty can of worms that I'd rather not deal with. I can just imagine Dad pacing around the kitchen at dawn, going on and on about how I should look before I leap. Then he'd drag us back to the airport and complain to the flunkies at Air Aloha, making a federal case out of it and embarrassing all of us in the process.

I try to remember what I had in the suitcase. Summer clothes that I'll outgrow by June. A bunch of shells that I wouldn't know what to do with anyway.

"Maybe I don't have to tell him," I suggest. "I mean ... maybe these clothes will fit."

"What, are you nuts? You're gonna wear someone else's clothes? What if they're diseased?"

I pull out a T-shirt. I don't recognize the design on the front. It's not a sports team or rock group or anything—just a weird swirl of colors. I sniff it to see if it's clean, and Leslie practically gags. "Oh how gross!" she says. They're clean . . . but there's something about them that smells kind of strange. It's like the way everyone's house has its own unique smell. I suppose clothes must be that way, too . . . but the scent on these clothes seems totally unfamiliar. I kind of like it, though.

I slip on the T-shirt. It fits perfectly, and the fabric feels softer than any other T-shirt I've worn.

"Problem solved," I announce. "I'll try on the rest of the clothes in the morning, and we don't have to tell anyone."

I can tell that Leslie's not too happy about the idea of taking someone else's bag. "When you think about it," I explain, "it's a fair exchange. Mine for theirs." I figure if they want theirs back, they can find us, but until then, I have a new set of clothes.

I turn, heading toward my bed, but Leslie stops me.

"Logan," she says, "don't move!"

I freeze. The last time she said that, there was this big Hawaiian tarantula crawling on my beach blanket. Leslie moves toward me from behind, and I feel something on my back. I go stiff, until I realize it's only Leslie's fingers, tickling my back.

"Ha ha, very funny," I say. But then I realize that although I have a shirt on, there's no fabric between her fingers and my back. She's tickling me through a hole in the shirt. A pretty big one, by my guess.

"Great," I say. "I get a cool shirt from someone else's suitcase and it has holes in it."

"It's not a hole, Logan," says Leslie. "I think you should look in the mirror."

I step into the bathroom, my back to the mirror, and crane my head as far as it will go, to get a glimpse of my back.

"Hmm . . . that's weird," I say. It's another sleeve. I try twisting my neck further, to get a better look at it. Finally I take the shirt off. There's no denying that my new shirt has a third sleeve.

"Maybe it's an irregular," suggests Leslie. "Mom always buys irregular T-shirts. They're cheaper."

Maybe. But somehow I find it hard to imagine a T-shirt company making that sort of mistake and still selling it to people. Then again, I've heard of big corporations trying to sell people toxic waste, so you never know.

"Yeah, maybe," I say. Then I put the shirt back on. Extra sleeve or not, it feels comfortable enough to sleep in. More than comfortable—it feels . . . right. And somehow I feel more content. So content that I slip right off to sleep.

Mom, in her maternal wisdom, lets us miss a day of school, so we can sleep in and catch up with Ohio time. I don't wake up until noon, and the first thing I do is head for the suitcase.

I pull out the shirts on top and hang them up. Problem is, the shirts don't fit properly on the hangers. Could be because they all have three sleeves.

I search for tags, and any other kinds of labels or logos that might tell me what the deal is, but all the tags have been cut out—just like my own clothes. Whoever owns these clothes doesn't like the tags scratching their neck either.

Beneath the shirt are the pants. My heart speeds up a bit as I pull a pair out, worried that I might find three legs. But no— the pants look normal. I try a pair on. They look like jeans, but the weave seems much finer. They don't fit as well as the shirt. Kind of baggy.

I reach down to zip up the fly and realize that there's no zipper. No button either. Sure, the fly's there, but there's nothing to hold it closed. Great. Here's one pair of pants I won't be wearing in public.

"How come you're wearing those backward?" Leslie says from the doorway. I turn to see her standing there, still half asleep.

"They're not backward," I inform her. "They just don't fit, gel-brain."

"Oh," she answers and yawns.

Leslie shuffles off to the bathroom, still too tired to match my rank-out. I hitch up the pants on my hips, then remember what Leslie said. I take off the pants and put them on the other way.

They fit perfectly.

In fact, they fit more comfortably than any other pants I own. See, Mom says I'm always in between sizes, which means that my pants are always either too tight or falling off my hips. But these feel like they were made for me.

Only one problem: Why is there a zipperless fly in the seat of my pants?

Well, there's an obvious answer—and in fact, I've often wondered why they don't make butt-zippers for that other all-important bathroom trip. But that couldn't be what this hole is for—it's a little too high for that.

But, like the shirt I wore last night, the pants feel *right*. So rather than worry about it, I make sure my three-sleeved shirt is out over the pants instead of tucked in. That way it covers the little hole and no one has to know it's there. No one has to know about my shirts either, if I wear a jacket over them.

As Leslie passes by, on her way back from the bathroom, I call her into my room.

"So, what do you think of my outfit?" I ask her.

"Great, if you like wearing stolen clothes."

"They're not stolen," I remind her, "just accidentally borrowed." And then I turn my back to her. "Will you scratch my back?" I ask.

Leslie reaches in through the third sleeve and scratches me between the shoulder blades—where it's been itching all night.

"Hey," she suggests, "maybe that's what the hole in the shirt is for—back-scratch access."

Which is as good an explanation as any. I don't tell her about the hole in the pants.

"Looks like you're getting a rash," says Leslie. "Your back's getting all lumpy."

"Must be something I caught in Hawaii," I tell her.

There's a fresh layer of snow on the ground, so I put on my coat and head out, taking two of the three gloves in the suitcase. It isn't until I try to make snowballs that I notice there's a space for a sixth finger.

An hour later, I'm back in my room with the suitcase. I just can't seem to get it out of my mind—but I don't talk to anyone about it, not even Leslie. I'm usually bad at keeping secrets—when weird things happen, I'm the first one to announce it to the world. But somehow this little piece of baggage has become a very personal and private thing. I guess everyone has things they don't want to share with their family. Sometimes it's just dumb things, and other times it's earth-shattering stuff. I try not to think about which category the suitcase falls into.

There are other things in the case, too. Silver coins that float up off your palm, as if they're filled with helium. A pen that writes with light instead of ink. In a side pocket, I find an electronic device that kind of looks like a Walkman, but the earphones don't quite fit in my ears. I wouldn't call the sounds that it plays music—it's more like clicks and screeches—but the more I listen to it, the more soothing it feels. It does have an interesting rhythm, in a way.

And then there's the can.

It's small and looks just like any other can of food, although there's no label. In a way it's the most disturbing thing of all, simply because it's normal. What would normal canned goods be doing mixed in with this stuff?

I can't sleep that night, mainly because of the way my hands and back itch, as if I'd fallen in a potent patch of poison ivy. But deep down I know it's not poison ivy at all. Instead of sleeping, I turn on my flashlight and take a long look at a picture I found in the suitcase's side pocket. There are people in the picture, and although the snapshot is a bit blurry, I can make out their faces. I suppose it's a family. Two parents, two kids. I don't know them, and yet I feel something for them, as if I did. I *want* to know them, but I can't say why.

Mom slips into my room, and I quickly hide the picture.

"I brought you a snack," she says, offering me a plate. "You barely touched your dinner. I thought you might be hungry."

"No thanks," I tell her. Truth is, I haven't had much of an appetite since we've gotten home from Maui.

Mom sees me rubbing my itching back against the wall, and she offers to scratch it for me, but I don't let her, because I know she'll see how the rash is swelling.

She looks at me strangely for a moment and asks, "Where'd you get those pajamas?"

"Hawaii," I tell her, which isn't a total lie. They are more comfortable than any pajamas I've ever worn—especially now, because I don't quite fit into my regular clothes anymore.

They've gotten tight in strange and unexpected places. I guess I'm having a growth spurt.

After Mom leaves, I finally fall asleep thinking of the people in the picture, and the little canister of food, which seems creepier the more I think about it.

The world changes forever the next day. Not the whole world, but the small part of it that I occupy. It starts with a fight—the kind of fight you have when you've packed day-old snow a little too tightly, so your snowball leaves a major raspberry on your friend's cheek when you throw it.

I hurl the ice-ball at Randy Small, because he threw one first. Problem is my throw is a lot stronger than Randy Small's. The ice-ball impacts on the side of his face, and he turns to me with eyes that scream schoolyard massacre. There's a dozen kids around us as Randy rushes me. He rams into me, and his momentum takes me down.

Randy's on the wrestling team, so it doesn't take long for him to pin me in the snow. As I look into his eyes, I can tell he's not about to use a wrestling move on me. Not unless loogie-hurl is an accepted wrestling maneuver. I struggle uselessly as he summons up a major midwinter-flu-season mass of phlegm, and then, before he can fire it at me, someone swings at him, punching him across the face with enough force to send him sprawling in the snow five feet away.

I look around to see who saved me but there's no one else close enough to have taken the shot.

Then I see my friends' eyes bug out. I see them back away. I see the hand that punched Randy Small. It's above my head, reaching down to flick some snow from my eyebrow. The hand—the arm, I realize, is mine.

Screaming, I tear off my coat. Although I can't see my back, I know what it looks like. There's an arm—looking just like my others—growing through the third sleeve in the middle of my back.

My friends all back away from me, then run.

"Wait!" I call after them. "Wait, I can explain." But I can't. Not really.

I feel something in the small of my back, too. Something growing out of that little backward fly. It's a tail, thin and curly, like the tail of a pig, and as I look at my gloves, I suddenly realize that the sixth finger-hole doesn't flop around limply anymore . . . because now there's something to fill it.

I race home screaming, trying to outrun my fear, but it follows behind me just as closely as my third arm.

It's dark. I've locked myself in my bathroom. Leslie keeps pounding, demanding to be let in, but I'm not opening the door for anyone. My parents don't know yet, but they will soon enough.

I tell myself that I didn't know what was happening, but that's a lie. Deep down, I knew. Maybe not at first, but somewhere along the way, I knew. And I guess I knew there was no way to stop it once it started. No matter how many two-sleeved shirts I put on, no matter how many five-fingered gloves, I would never be the way I was. Because the new clothes felt *right*.

On the counter in front of me is the can. Although it looks like any old can of tuna fish, I know there's no tuna inside. I know it without having to look. I hook on an old can opener and turn the crank. It turns in a slow circle, and I laugh, because it reminds me of the airport carousel that began this new chapter of my life.

I don't know why the suitcase chose me, but it did. Or maybe it was just dumb luck. Anyway, it doesn't matter now. As I turn the can opener with my other two arms, I bend my third elbow and press my new arm firmly against my back. I suppose we could move someplace, where no one knows about it. I could hide it in normal shirts, covered by bulky sweaters. Or maybe I could lock myself away in a basement somewhere, where no one can see. Maybe. But right now, I can't even think beyond tonight, and telling my parents. How do you tell your parents something like this—something that will change the way they see you forever?

The can opener makes a full circle, and I pull open the lid. I knew it. I knew it because I heard them. In the dead of the night I heard them moving inside the can.

Blue, wormlike things—hundreds of them sliding over one another, trying to hide from the light. I know I should be disgusted, but "knowing" and "being" are two different things. And the fact is, I haven't lost my appetite. I simply haven't been hungry for the food in the kitchen. I didn't know what I was hungry for until just now ... although I did have a sneaking suspicion. That's why I brought a spoon.

They arrive the next day. Something told me that they would. So I pack a suitcase. I watch with Leslie and my parents as they land on our lawn in a ship that seems to me what a minivan might look like, if GM built them for interstellar travel instead of rush hour gridlock. Leslie cries silently, and my parents, well, they're still locked in the same shock they've been in since last night. Either they've accepted it or they're denying any of this is happening; I can't say which.

As I stride forward, suitcase in my third hand, the boy carrying my old suitcase steps forward as well, and we meet in the middle of the lawn. He's wearing my old Cleveland Indians shirt and my favorite jeans. He only has two hands with five fingers on each, but I know that's not the way he started. He started looking much like his family standing by the van.

"Hi," he says.

"Hi," I say back, and turn to take a look at my old family. "They're okay," I tell him. "You'll learn to love them."

But he just grins at me. I realize then that his English stops at the word hi. I suppose both of us will be learning new languages.

We look at each other for a moment more. He seems pleasant enough. We probably could have been friends, if circumstances were different. But now all we can do is pass each other as I move into the arms of his family, and he moves into the arms of mine.

My new father smiles at me, speaking strangely. He greets me by clasping my third hand above our heads, in a sort of bizarre high-five. My new mother smiles, and my new kid brother offers me a fresh can of food.

As I look at the worms squirming in the can, something suddenly strikes me as very funny. "Wow, what a nasty can of worms this is, huh?" I say, and laugh long and loud. My new family laughs as well, but they have no idea what they're laughing about. That's okay.

As I get into the van and strap myself in, my new brother hands me a book. On the first page is a picture of an odd-looking fruit.

⅂ is for ⅂⅃⇑

Okay. I'll deal with this. Somehow I'll find a way to deal with this, I know I will.

My dad always said that life is like a game of poker. I suppose you learn to live with the hand you're dealt. Even when it's three of a kind.

Where they came from . . .

I often get asked what planet I was on when I wrote a particular story. Well, rest assured, it was good old Mother Earth . . . at least I think it was. In any case, here are sparks of ideas that led to each of the stories in *MindStorms*.

Pacific Rim

I'd always been intrigued by paintings I'd seen of ships falling off the edge of the Earth. Recently, I received a brochure in the mail, advertizing the largest cruise ship in the world—truly magnificent to behold—and it occurred to me that the only thing more bizarre than old sailing ships falling off the edge of the Earth, would be a giant cruise ship suffering the same fate . . . but if you think the story is far-fetched, consider the fact that there are actually people living in our modern society who support the idea of a flat Earth! In fact, in the 1930's a guy by the name of Wilbur Glenn Voliva offered $5000 to anyone who could prove that the world was round. The weird thing is, that he never had to pay out a cent. Talk about truth being stranger than fiction.

I of the Storm

It was the windiest night of the year. Papers flew through the air, trash cans rolled down the street. It was as if the wind had a personality, and was having . . . a tantrum. That thought hit me at about one in the morning, and kept me awake until I finally dragged myself out of bed before dawn and began to write this story.

Opabinia

My son had to give a first-grade report on an animal. Of all things, he chose the weird, extinct Opabinia—something I had never heard of. We went on the Internet to do some research, and were dazzled by the amazing history of the Burgess Shale—and that if the creatures of the Cambrian period didn't die off, we might look very different than we do now. . . .

Dawn Terminator

It occurred to me some time ago, that if the Sun were to start pouring lethal radiation out over the world, the people on the dark side of the Earth wouldn't know until the sun rose. And then it occurred to me that there are places where you could escape from sunlight, if you really had to. . . .

Midnight Michelangelo

I can't take full credit for this one. The concept was originally the "brain-child" of writer Terry Black, before I got my "ten-tacles" on it. We developed the story together as a short film script, because sometimes two brains are better than one, and I liked it so much, I decided to write it as a short story.

Ralphy Sherman's Inside Story

Ralphy's rapidly becoming my favorite character. He makes a cameo appearance in just about all of my novels, and this is the second story that he stars in. He is the master of exaggerations, tall tales, and bald-faced lies, which opens quite a few possi-bilities for stories, because in Ralphy's world, the more im-probable an event, the more likely he is to swear it really happened. As to where I got the idea for this particular story, to be honest, I haven't got a clue. Maybe I blocked it out.

He Opens a Window

When I was in high school, I had this thing about painting windows that open up to other worlds. In fact, when I was in college, I painted a few windows-on-other-worlds murals. But the illustrator came up with the cover for this book without knowing any of that. When I saw the cover sketch, it inspired me to come up with a story, and I began to consider who, more than anyone else, might need to escape through such a window. I only wish such a window could exist, and that there were millions of windows like it.

Clothes Make the Man

I am no stranger to luggage troubles. A certain airline, which shall remain nameless, shattered my laptop computer, and at a different time, shredded a brand-new piece of luggage. Have you ever noticed when you travel, that there's always one or two pieces of luggage left going around the carousel that no one claims. Ever wonder who they might belong to? I do.

Brrrrrrr. . .

It sure got cold fast, didn't it?
But that's just the way it is in *MindStorms*.
Because even though it may be blue skies outside,
inside it's stormy weather. . . .

The forecast?

Who knows for sure?
But it looks like another storm coming.
So zip up your raincoat. And hold on tight.
You're about to be blown away.

Don't miss *MindQuakes: Stories to Shatter Your Brain* and other titles in this exciting series from award-winner Neal Shusterman.